FIRST DATE

"Hello, again." Austin smiled over at me as he started the car. He looked great tonight in an emerald-colored sweater that made his eyes look even greener.

He maneuvered his car smoothly onto the freeway, driving a little too fast. "Gotta change our plans for tonight. I finally found an apartment and started moving today." He reached over and took my hand. "I'd like you to help."

"Sure." I slouched down in the seat and wondered what my mom would say if she knew I'd be spending the evening at a guy's apartment. I felt panicky, like the date was out of my control. I wanted to be back home, where it was safe . . .

I've Got Your Number

Dian Curtis Regan

AN AVON FLARE BOOK

For John

I'VE GOT YOUR NUMBER is an original publication of Avon Books.
This work has never before appeared in book form.

AVON BOOKS
A division of
The Hearst Corporation
1790 Broadway
New York, New York 10019

Copyright © 1986 by Dian Curtis Regan
Published by arrangement with the author
Library of Congress Catalog Card Number: 85-91531
ISBN: 0-380-75082-1
RL: 5.3

First Flare Printing: July 1986

FLARE TRADEMARK REG. U. S. PAT. OFF. AND IN
OTHER COUNTRIES. MARCA REGISTRADA, HECHO EN
U.S.A.

Printed in the U.S.A.

K–R   10 9 8 7 6 5 4 3 2 1

Chapter 1

It was the end of summer vacation. My best friend, Angel Killion, and I had just given up our final, desperate attempt at getting the gorgeous tans we'd been trying to get all summer long.

We packed away our swimsuits for the last time, got dressed, and headed down the street to MacKenzie's to get something to eat. It was then I felt the apprehension start.

I'd gotten braces put on my teeth during the summer and this would be the first time anyone would see the new me—metallic Emily Crocker. I was feeling extremely self-conscious about the whole thing.

Maybe it wasn't too late to turn around and save the unavoidable, embarrassing moment for tomorrow—the first day of school.

Killion shot me an exasperated look. "Crocker, why are you walking so slow? Hurry it up. It's tradition for everyone to show up at MacKenzie's the day before school starts." We call each other by our last names because our first names are not exactly ones we would have picked for ourselves.

I made a last-minute attempt to change our destination. "Killion, why are we going out for a pizza, anyway? What about your diet?"

"This is my last week of freedom. I'm going to come up with a new diet plan, start on it Saturday, and be skinny by November."

I smiled at her lovable inconsistency.

As we suspected, MacKenzie's was packed. It was impossible not to smile and reveal my braces. Therefore, a

lot of people got their cute comments in ahead of time as
we plowed our way to an empty booth in the back.

Before doing anything else, I slipped over to the jukebox and selected my favorite song to play three times in a
row. The melody followed me back to the booth:

"I learned the truth at seventeen,
that love was meant for beauty queens,
and high school girls with clear-skinned smiles,
who married young and then retired. . . ."

"Crocker, you're going to wear out that record if you
keep playing it over and over," Killion groaned as she
tossed me a menu.

"I identify with it," I said, trying to sound dramatic.
"I'm going to suffer through my youth just like it says in
the song."

"You're not even seventeen yet."

"So, I'll be good at suffering by then. I've got two
years to practice." I tossed the menu back to her. "I think
you should start identifying with my song too, Killion, and
throw out all those drippy romance novels you've been
devouring all summer."

She'd talked me into reading one or two of her romances,
and I knew right away that the girls in those books were
not the Crockers and Killions of the world.

"But," she protested, pushing up her glasses, "the girls
in those stories always solve all their problems and wind
up with a terrific boyfriend by the end of the book. I'm
just trying to figure out how they do it."

I rolled my eyes as she continued. "It gives me hope to
read those books, and I learn a lot about how to talk to
guys and how to act around them—if I ever get the oppor-
tunity, that is. At least I'm not accepting my fate like
you're doing with that song."

She left to order a pizza while I leaned back in the
booth to think about our list of self-improvements we'd
made up the day after school was out in June. It looked
something like this:

GOALS FOR THE SUMMER

Purpose: to attract boys

CROCKER	KILLION
Build up body (too skinny)	Lose twenty-five pounds
Spend time in the sun to:	Get contact lenses
clear up complexion	Learn how to apply makeup
sun-bleach boring brown	to:
hair	maximize brown eyes
Get a gorgeous tan	(hidden under glasses)
Let hair grow long	Get a gorgeous tan
Learn how to apply makeup	Do *something* with long hair
to:	(too dark brown to
minimize braces and	sun-bleach)
blemishes	
maximize pale blue eyes	

I thought I'd be a blond, tanned goddess by summer's end, but miracles must take longer than a mere three months. And Killion had ended up gaining weight over the summer instead of losing it.

Getting contact lenses had been a great idea—especially since she'd gotten a part-time job at the mall to pay for them. But her dad, Reverend Killion, had been against it. He'd said, "Angel, you're far too concerned about externals when it's the internals that count." She decided later that a good answer would have been, "Guys don't ask out your internals, they ask out your externals."

The words to the song "At Seventeen" broke into my thoughts again:

"And those of us with ravaged faces,
lacking in the social graces,
desperately remained at home
inventing lovers on the phone. . . ."

"I suspected you were here when I heard that song."
Startled, I looked up to see Kevin, my older brother. He

is seventeen, a senior, and strange as it may seem, my second best friend.

"I'll give you a ride home," he said. "I've got the car."

"You're kidding!" I exclaimed. "Dad actually let you take the car?"

Our mom was due to have a baby any minute, and Dad didn't want it to happen while his kids were off in the family car. The unexpected addition to our household had been quite a surprise at first, but now we were all eagerly looking forward to the event.

Kevin waved good-bye to some friends who were on their way out the door and continued, "It took a lot of persuading, but Dad finally agreed after I wrote down MacKenzie's number and left it by the phone."

Killion returned and Kevin slid into the booth next to her, taking a sip of my Coke. "Hey, Kill," he began, "did you hear the joke about the pencil?"

"No."

"Oh, forget it. There's no point to it."

Without missing a beat, Killion joined in. "Did you hear the one about the rope?"

"No."

"Oh, skip it."

I closed my eyes and tuned them out. That's the way it usually went when the three of us got together—bad jokes and puns, with me feeling a little left out. I used to think it'd be great if those two started dating, but the older we got, the more I realized that all they'd ever be is friends. As a matter of fact, it was Danny, Kevin's best friend, who I suspected Killion had a secret crush on.

I watched Kevin double over at Killion's last joke. (Did you hear the one about the roof? Oh, forget it. It's over your head.) He'd gotten all the looks in the family, complete with dark, curly hair, and the "clear-skinned smile" I should have inherited. It wasn't fair to have such a tall, good-looking brother. Kevin had been on a health kick since midsummer, so he joined our self-improvement program, then took up weight lifting and jogging.

"Hey, Emily!" yelled some girl I barely knew. "What's with the railroad tracks?" She pointed to her teeth.

I could feel Kevin and Killion watching me to see how I was going to react to the comment. Secretly I was ecstatic that my teeth would be picket-fence perfect in a couple of years, but publicly I rather enjoyed playing a martyr.

I gave them a halfhearted smile. "These are supposed to be the best years of my life, and no guy is ever going to kiss me until I'm ninety-five years old."

"That's not true, Em," Kevin said as the pizza arrived. "I dated Loni Ames a few times and she wore braces. Remember?"

"So, what was it like kissing her?"

"I . . . uh . . . well, I don't know. I never kissed her."

"See?"

"Look, idiot." He reached across the table, grabbed me by the hair, and stuffed three napkins into my mouth. "It wasn't because she wore braces, believe me. It was because she wouldn't let me kiss her."

"With a body like Loni Ames's, and all that long, black hair to set it off," Killion mumbled, "a guy's not going to notice a little thing like braces."

"Thanks, friend," I sputtered, pulling the napkins out of my mouth.

We attacked the pizza, then turned our attention to the couple who'd just walked in. Both had shiny blond hair, perfectly in place, and were dressed like they were modeling for *Seventeen*.

"How come the best-looking girl in the class always ends up with the best-looking guy?" Killion asked. "Stacy Benson and Stan Jenson. I think one of them should change their name. That's just too cute." She looked slyly at Kevin and continued, "Hey, didn't you ask Stacy out once?"

"Me?" He tried to deny it. "Why would I want to date a girl with an IQ the same as her age?" He took a giant bite of pizza so he wouldn't have to explain any further.

The battle of the wits was on again.

"She turned you down, huh?" Killion laughed. "That's okay, I heard that Stan gave her a book for a birthday present, and she couldn't figure out where to put the batteries.''

Halfway through our meal, a sudden loud voice boomed across the restaurant, ''PHONE CALL FOR EMILY CROCKER!''

The restaurant grew unusually quiet as I rose and tried to float invisibly up to the front counter through a stream of ''Hi, Emilys,'' and ''Hey, Crockers.'' My face grew hot with embarrassment.

It was Dad. ''Hon, it's time. I knew this would happen.''

I pictured his tall, lanky form hunched over the phone in the hallway and knew he was tugging on his beard the way he always did when he was nervous.

''Get the car home as quickly as you can.''

Hanging up the phone, I motioned to Kevin and Killion, who'd already figured it out and were on their way up to meet me. The three of us flew out the front amid curious stares. At the door, Killion called back over her shoulder, ''We're gonna have a baby!''

Chapter 2

The first day of school was little more than a haze to me after staying up half the night waiting to hear from my dad. He finally called about 3:30 in the morning to tell me I had a new baby sister.

I didn't even know what her name was because they hadn't picked one out yet. All I knew was that Dad had suggested we call her "Caboose," since she was the last one in line. I hoped he was kidding.

I got home from school just as Kevin was leaving for a job interview. He'd decided to get a part-time job to save for his own car.

The house was empty, so I decided to make my own dinner. My mom had strongly requested that I not use the stove when I'm home alone since I'd started two small kitchen fires last summer. It wasn't my fault the phone rang at the wrong time.

Anyway, I have the worst reputation in the world as a cook, so just to play it safe, I popped a bagel into the microwave oven.

At that instant, the telephone rang. Doesn't matter which oven I'm using, I thought as I answered it.

"Hon? This is Dad. Just wanted to see if you made it home from school all right. I'll come get you and take you back to the hospital to see Mom and the baby. Okay?"

"Sure, Dad. What does she look like?"

"Mom? Oh, she's tall, and has short, brown hair. . . . ."

"No, Dad." I groaned. "What does the *baby* look like?"

7

"Well, to be honest with you, she looks a little bit like Great-Grandfather Crocker."

"Dad! That's terrible!"

He laughed. "Wait until you meet her, Em. She's so smart. Why, just a minute after she was born, she'd already learned how to cry."

"Oh, Dad." I groaned again. "You're getting worse than Kevin. What's her name?"

"Who? Caboose Crocker?"

"You didn't!" I yelled at him. "You wouldn't!"

"Calm down, Hon. Just kidding. Her name is Wendy Lynn. Is that better?"

"That's great. I like it. I'll be ready when you get here."

I hung up and dialed Killion's number with one hand while I opened the microwave with the other, and stared at a dead bagel. I must have punched in ten minutes instead of ten seconds. Picking it up, I sailed it across the room toward the trash can. It sounded like it weighed ninety-five pounds when it landed. The goof-up gourmet strikes again, I thought.

"Helllooo?"

Killion always says "Hello" in a slow, sexy voice just in case it is a guy calling. She'd been practicing it for over a year now and hadn't had a chance to impress anyone yet.

I crooned into the phone. "Don't waste it on me, dahling!"

"Oh, Crocker, it's only you."

"Sorry to disappoint you. Just wanted to tell you that my new sister's name, thankfully, is Wendy."

"Wendy? I love it. How come all the other girls get the cute names? Wendy, Stacy, Loni. Why did we get passed by?"

"We're going to change our names, remember? I've thought it over, and I have mine picked out. Are you ready, Killion?"

"Hit me with it."

"Tarrah," I drawled, with feeling. "With two *r*'s and an *h*. What do you think?"

"I think you won't be able to marry Michael Farrah

because then your name would be Tarrah Farrah. That sounds like a city in Indonesia.''

"Right," I agreed. "Well, if Michael Farrah wanted to marry me, I'd change my name back again. As a matter of fact, he can call me anything he wants to.''

"How about if he calls you tomorrow?" she teased.

I laughed. Even the thought of him calling gave me goose bumps. "So what are you changing your name to?''

"I've narrowed it down to two—Soozi with two *o*'s and a *z*, or Dawne with an *e*. What do you think?''

I hesitated, not wanting to hurt her feelings. "I think I'd stick to Angel with an *l*. . . .''

"Thanks, friend," she grumbled. "You're right. You can't have a cute name like that unless you have a pert little cheerleader body. Well, back to the baby name books.''

No sooner had I hung up the phone when it rang again. I glanced at the clock. Now I wouldn't have time for dinner. "Hello?" I knew my voice sounded a little irritated.

"Hello?" said a wonderfully masculine voice on the other end. It definitely was not Kevin's friend Danny.

"Helllooo!" I said again, trying Killion's method this time.

He sounded uncertain. "I was trying to call Rene Crocker. Is this the right number?''

"Is that Renee with two *e*'s?" I was fascinated by his soft voice but knew immediately that was a really stupid thing to say.

He laughed. "Maybe it's even Renée with two *e*'s and one of those little accent marks, too. I don't know. Does it matter?''

"No, it really doesn't.''

"Is this Rene?''

"No, it isn't.''

"Is she there?''

"No. You have the wrong number.''

"What?" He sounded surprised. "Why are you giving me such a hard time if I'm calling the wrong number?''

We laughed together. It sounded wonderful.

"With whom do I have the pleasure of speaking?" he asked formally.

My dad's warning of never giving out my name or any information over the phone flashed through my mind. But this guy had obviously just been looking through the list of Crockers in the phone book, trying to find the one he knew. I decided he had a voice I could trust.

"This is *Emily* Crocker."

"Is that Emily with a *y?*" he teased.

"Yes, Emily with a *y*." We laughed again. Talking to him was so easy!

Suddenly I became aware of my dad honking the horn for me. "Um, I have to hang up now. Nice talking to you." Stupid comment number two, I thought.

"Oh, Emily Crocker?" His voice was so fantastic.

"Yes?"

"May I call you again sometime? Just to talk?"

"Well, I . . ." My dad was really laying on the horn now. "Sure. Please call again. 'Bye!"

I hung up the phone and flew out the door. I don't think my feet touched the ground.

Chapter 3

"He actually asked if he could call you again and you said yes?"

Killion leaned over so she could see my face as we walked to school the next morning. I shrugged at her question.

"So, what's his name?"

"I don't know," I said, trying to act casual.

"You didn't ask his name? Not even after he asked yours?"

I shook my head no as I flipped a fallen leaf off my shoulder.

"This is great." She giggled as she did a little hop-step on the sidewalk. "This is even better than some of my romance novels. The Mystery Caller. I can't wait until he calls again."

"*You* can't wait," I exclaimed, catching up with her. "*I* can't wait. I wonder what kind of a face goes with such a sexy voice? He should be a disc jockey—his voice was that great."

"Have you told Kevin yet? He'll crack up!"

"No. Oh, speaking of Kevin, he got the job he interviewed for. He's now a movie director."

"A movie director?" she asked with disbelief as she adjusted her glasses. "How could he get a job like that? Especially in this town?"

I couldn't help laughing. "He's a movie director—he directs people to their seats at the movies."

"Oh, brother. That had to be Kevin's joke, right?"

"You're right," I answered. "I'm not that original. I

guess I can't even steal a joke from my brother without getting caught.''

The second day of school was a lot more relaxing for me. I'd stopped feeling like I was all braces and was able to calm down and even smile every once in a while. Most of the comments had been encouraging. (''It's neat that you're getting your teeth straightened. I wish I could.'') And there had only been a few wisecrackers calling me names like ''Tinsel Teeth'' or ''Metal Mouth.'' I'd spent most of study hall in the rest room practicing how to smile without showing my teeth. I had it down pretty well by the end of the period.

Michael Farrah turned up in my English class, which put some excitement into my life. I'd had a crush on him for about ninety-five years. Every time he looked at me with those beautiful blue eyes, my insides turned into marshmallow. We said ''hello'' and talked about assignments and school in general, but that was about the extent of our friendship. I didn't have the nerve to sit next to him, so I sat a few rows behind him and a couple over. At least I could stare at the back of his wavy blond hair.

After lunch I stopped by the girls' room. Loni Ames was applying her twentieth coat of mascara as she gave Stacy Benson some advice which I wish I'd heard the day before. She had about three sticks of gum in her mouth, so in between chompings, she said breathlessly: ''What you do, Stace, is this. (Chomp, chomp.) You walk into a new class on the first day of school, pause at the door, and casually scan the room. Guys get to class before girls, right? Because they don't stop off to comb their hair and fix their makeup and all that. So (chomp, chomp) you pick out the best-looking guy and take the desk either in front of him or next to him. In back is not as good, but it's better than nothing. Okay? But you make it look like it wasn't planned. That way, for the rest of the semester you're not staring across the room at the best-looking guy while being surrounded by creeps. You're right there for him to talk to. (Chomp, chomp.) In front of him is definitely the best place, because then only you can hear his comments during class, and if he sees you laughing, he'll love you. Guys *love* it when you laugh at their jokes. So anyway (chomp, chomp) the best way to start it off is to ask him if he has an extra pen. . . ."

Her voice trailed off as they left the room. I resisted the urge to follow them so I could listen to the rest of the advice. Why hadn't I thought of that the day before when I walked into English and immediately saw Michael Farrah sitting by himself? He's not going to chitchat with a girl who sits three rows behind him and two rows over. And how can I borrow a pen when I'm that far away?

After school I ran most of the way to my house. Mom had come home from the hospital and I'd really missed her—especially her cooking. Dad had taken over in the kitchen instead of me. It was a little embarrassing. I decided to add "Learn to Cook" to my list of self-improvements and extend the deadline a few more months.

I tiptoed into the guest-room-turned-nursery and was greeted by the smell of baby powder. Mom was sitting in a chair by the window, her hair pulled back on the sides with a pair of my barrettes. She was nursing Wendy.

"Hi, Mom, you look great," I whispered, wishing again I'd inherited her good looks instead of Kevin. "Missed you," I said, kissing her on the cheek.

"Hi, Em." She smiled at me. "I've missed you, too, but you don't have to whisper. She's not asleep, she just finished her dinner." Mom handed the bundle to me carefully so she could button her blouse.

I cradled my new sister in the crook of my arm. "She's so tiny and pink. Uh, oh." I ran my hand over the dark, curly fuzz on top of her head. "If she gets Kevin's hair I'll never speak to her."

Kevin stuck his head in the door. "She's not getting my hair. I won't give it to her." His friend Danny was with him. He was the same height as Kevin, only a lot more muscular, with auburn hair and brown eyes.

Wendy gazed up at me. I gingerly handed her back to Mom as I crooned at her, "Hi, Wendy, I'm your big sister, Emily. Do you remember being born?"

"Naw," Kevin answered, "I was too young."

"I wasn't talking to you." I groaned, turning my attention to Danny. "Remember how big your little brother was when he was born?"

"Yeah," he answered, "he looked like he could have played quarterback by the time he was three months old."

"Are you two boys ever serious?" Mom smiled, shaking her head. She stood up and carried Wendy over to the crib. "Come here and I'll teach you all how to change a diaper."

"Time to leave," Kevin announced. "I'm a male chauvinist with a capital *S*."

"Capital *C*," I corrected him.

Danny paused at the door. "Hey, Wendy, you and I have a date in fifteen years. Pick you up at eight!"

Mom laughed as she opened a fresh box of diapers. "I can't wait until Wendy starts talking to see if she's going to take after Kevin. Then, if it's not too late, we could always trade her in for a normal kid, like my Emily."

Normal kid, I thought later as I lay on my bed, reading. Is that what Mom thinks about me? I didn't want to spend my life excelling in normal. It's not that I wanted to be Supergirl either. I just wanted to be good at one thing. Stacy was artistic. Loni was an actress. Killion was clever and witty. It seemed like everyone had at least one specialty—except me.

I lived in fear that a guy was going to ask me out (finally) to a swim party and find out that not only couldn't I swim, but I was also afraid of the water. Or he'd ask me out to play tennis, and I didn't even know how to hold a racket. Or, what if a guy asked me to go skiing? I'd never be able to get up the hill in the first place because I'm terrified of chair lifts. I've never been on one before, but I know I'd die suspended high up off the ground on a little dinky cable. And how do you get onto the stupid things? In skis, no less. They don't even stop!

What if the Mystery Caller asks me out? What kind of a date would I be good at? Movies? I'm good at movies. I don't have to do anything. Plus, it'd be too dark for him to see my braces or my complexion. On the other hand, I always choke when I eat popcorn, so I drink a Coke to wash it down, and usually end up with the hiccups. Then, what if he tried to hold my hand? One of them would be greasy from the popcorn and the other one would be cold and sticky from the Coke. I can't even do movies!

Forget about a dinner date. I always get really self-conscious trying to eat around guys. I hate it when they sit at our table in the cafeteria at school. My stomach knots up and I don't feel like eating at all.

So my mom thinks I'm normal—ha! Wonder what the Mystery Caller will think?

Chapter 4

"So, we've almost survived the first week of school," Killion announced as we started home on Thursday afternoon. A crisp wind hinted that fall was arriving early.

Hugging a pile of books, I matched Killion's pace. "I can't believe I daydreamed my way through every class this week."

"Still thinking about the Mystery Caller? Has he called again?"

"No." I felt dejected. "Why did he ask if he could call again, then not do it? Doesn't he know I'm the girl he could possibly be dying to go steady with?"

"Hey, Crocker, just because a guy says he's going to call you on the phone, doesn't mean he's going to give you a ring!"

"Did that have a double meaning, or what?"

She grinned and stopped to pet a spotted dog, which hurried on down the sidewalk. "Listen, I've got great plans for us this weekend while all the other girls are doing boring things, such as going out on dates."

"Okay, shoot."

"First, we go out on Friday after school, buy some magazines and check out some books from the library that deal with the problems on our list of self-improvements. We read them Friday night. I sleep over. Then we go out shopping on Saturday for clothes, makeup, banana splits—"

"Banana splits?"

"I just threw that in to see if you were listening."

"Sounds like a whoopee Friday night to me."

"What else did you have planned?"

"Good point," I muttered, hopping off the curb to walk in the street. "Wait a minute. How come you always invite yourself over to sleep at my house?"

"Oh, Crocker, your parents are so neat. Mine are too strict."

"That's ridiculous."

"No it isn't. You know my dad won't even let me have friends over to our house."

I gave her a sympathetic look. It seemed like her father vetoed every plan she made and was always laying down long lists of rules for her to follow. I knew she felt stifled at home. "Okay," I said, patting her on the shoulder. "I think it's a great plan."

After school on Friday, we walked to the drugstore and picked out a bunch of magazines on health, fashion, exercise, skin care, and hair styles. Then we tromped over to the library to check out some books on the same subjects.

"As long as we're out getting all this hateful exercise," huffed Killion, leaning against a fence to catch her breath, "why don't we stop off at MacKenzie's to pick up a pizza for later?"

"But your diet . . ."

"I'm starting it tomorrow, Crock. I've still got until midnight tonight. Besides, I can always drink a diet pop with the pizza, okay?"

We took a detour, ending up at MacKenzie's. While we were waiting for our pizza (we ordered hot fudge sundaes to kill the time) Michael Farrah walked in with some friends. I tried not to look as he passed our booth, but I couldn't help glancing up at him at the last instant. For a few seconds those blue eyes locked together with mine as he nodded and waved.

"Killion!" I hissed. "Did you see that? He waved to me! Out in public! I don't believe it!" I got so excited I choked on my ice cream. I tried to cough as gracefully as I could.

Killion leaned across the table. "Wouldn't it be great," she said in a low voice, "if Michael Farrah was your Mystery Caller?" She tilted her sundae dish to get the last drop of ice cream.

"Sure." I raised my head and made a face at her. "That'd be too much of a coincidence. That's something that would happen to one of those Stacy girls in the romance novels you read. Except girls like Stacy don't need to read books like that because they live lives like that."

"Not true," Killion argued. "I saw the book *Fiery Dreams* sitting on Stacy's desk in study hall."

"She probably wrote it," I muttered, licking some stray chocolate off my fingers.

Killion ignored me and continued, "Here's my theory. Let's say that one or two years ago, Stacy looked just like me, okay? Then she started reading romance novels, and they changed her whole life—like they're changing mine."

"They make you eat hot fudge sundaes?"

"No, Crocker, just listen. Let's say that Stacy was transformed from a nobody like me into what she is now—outgoing, pretty, great figure, and popular with the guys." Killion leaned in closer. "She probably had a first name she hated too, and in the process of change, she dropped it, and became Stacy, the goddess. Her name could have been Lucretia or something awful like that."

I couldn't help laughing at her sincerity.

"Ah, ha, Crocker. You laugh now, but if you don't keep up with me I'll leave you in the dust." She patted the stack of resource material we'd collected. "That reminds me of something else, *Tarrah*," she continued. "Let's try out our new names tonight." She held out her hand. "Meet Ginger. Ginger Killion."

"Hey, that one I like." We shook hands.

"PICK UP PIZZA FOR ANGEL KILLION!" boomed a loud voice over the intercom.

"It's *Ginger* Killion," she retorted.

Chapter 5

By the time we'd spread out the books, magazines, and pizza in my tiny bedroom, there was barely any space left for us. We each dug out a comfortable spot and spent the rest of the evening reading articles and skimming through books, taking notes here and there.

I had myself convinced I'd hear from the Mystery Caller some time during the evening since it was Friday night, so I was disappointed when he didn't call. I sure hoped Killion didn't think I'd made him up.

The articles on skin and hair care were fascinating to me. Killion was into the diet and makeup books. It was two o'clock in the morning before we finally turned out the light and fell asleep, with visions of fashion models twirling through our heads.

Our first stop at the mall the next day was the Scissor Shop. We each had a private consultation with a hair specialist, then ordered "the works." Michelle, who worked on me, "painted" small strands of my hair a sunny blond color. During the process I got very nervous, but the results were fantastic. I couldn't take my eyes off the blond who stared back at me from the mirror. What a difference!

I glided over to where Peter was putting the finishing touches on Killion, and watched him trim her bangs so they feathered back on the sides, slimming down her face.

When they were through with us, we floated through the mall, heading for the cosmetic counter in the department store, where, Peter had told us, we could get a free make-over and manicure.

I watched the cosmetologist, Mrs. French, working wonders on Killion while her assistant manicured my nails. Then it was my turn for a make-over. We switched places and the same procedures were repeated on me.

The results were startling. Killion swore that it made her look at least six days older, and I thought we both looked gorgeous—for us, that is.

We bought some makeup, then shopped around for accessories, since our research pointed out that accessories could "wake up a tired wardrobe." We decided our wardrobes were more dead than tired. Besides, we didn't have enough money to buy new clothes.

I bought a cookbook for beginners and some "problem skin" medication. Killion's major purchase was a pair of new glasses, since her dad had said "no" to contacts.

As we headed out into the mall, I searched through all the unfamiliar faces in the passing crowd, wondering if one of them could be my Mystery Caller.

"Every time I come to the mall, I see ninety-five people I know," I grumbled, "and usually want to hide. Now I want to be seen and no one's here."

"I know who we can go visit." Killion grabbed my arm and pulled me toward the escalator. "I want you to meet my boss, Mr. Lebowitz."

The card and gift shop where Killion worked was almost empty, even though it was a weekend. Mr. Lebowitz, a large, sad-looking man without one single hair on top of his head, leaned forlornly against the cash register, hairy arms folded across his chest. He didn't recognize Killion at first.

"Mr. Lebowitz? Hi! It's me, Angel Killion. This is the friend I was telling you about, Emily Crocker."

"Angel? Look at you!" His thick New York accent was appealing. "You're gorgeous. And Miss Emily, pleased to meet you." A huge hairy hand took hold of mine and shook it briskly. "How are you?"

"Fine, Mr. Lebowitz," I answered politely. "How's business?"

"Ay, business!" He put a hand on his head. "Business is so bad, my son-in-law got the brilliant idea to sell flowers, hoping it'd bring in more customers.'' He waved his arm toward a wall of plants. "Now I've got plenty of green around, but none of it's in the cash register.''

Killion and I exchanged looks. "Well, we'd better get going.'' She backed toward the door.

"Nice to meet you, Mr. Lebowitz.'' I waved to him as I followed her. He called after us, "I tell ya, girls, if I had any hair, it'd be turning gray right now . . .''

We giggled all the way home. Of course we made sure we regained our composure every time we heard a car approaching. Then we'd strike poses as if we were models. We got two honks and three whistles, which was great for our egos. I hadn't felt this terrific in a long time. I wondered how long it was going to last.

Arriving back at my house, Killion and I made our grand entrance. Danny was there with Kevin. Everyone stopped and stared, looking us over from head to toe. We dropped our packages and did a few of our model poses, now that we were good at them.

Danny and Killion stayed for dinner, and I couldn't help noticing how much Danny stared at her. I was dying to find out if she'd noticed it, too, but I couldn't ask her without the others hearing. She was the first one finished with the sparse helpings she'd taken and she waited patiently for everyone else, politely passing up dessert. Leaning toward me she whispered, "Eating makes me hungry.''

"Oh, Ginger.'' I laughed.

Mom gave me a funny look. "Emily, why did you just call Angel 'Ginger'?''

"I did?'' I tried to look as innocent as I could. "I don't know. I must have made a mistake.''

"We have a cat named Ginger,'' Danny commented to no one in particular.

I had to hold my breath to keep from laughing.

Usually the weekends passed too quickly, but this time I couldn't wait for it to be over. On Sunday night I carefully picked out something to wear to school the next day. It was only my brown cords with a tan sweater, but now I knew how to "wake it up" with accessories.

As I turned out the light and climbed into bed, I couldn't help feeling like I used to on the night before Christmas. I just couldn't wait to see everyone's reaction at school to the "new me." Please notice, Michael Farrah. . . .

Chapter 6

Monday morning I woke up feeling miserable. My whole body ached, my head was pounding, and I was shivering. I dragged myself to the mirror. My eyes were puffy and my face had turned red from the medication I'd put on it the night-before. "Mom!" I yelled weakly and fell back into bed, moaning into my pillow, "Not today . . ."

"Em, what is it?" She took one look at me and knew. "Oh, no. Your dad has the same thing. You'll both have to stay home today."

At first I felt dejected about staying home on what I'd hoped was going to be a special day. But it wasn't the total waste of time I'd thought it would be. I spent hours reading more of the books and magazine articles on health, diet, and exercise. Many of the articles emphasized that inner health affected outer beauty. This idea interested me so much that I asked Mom to bring me a pile of envelopes, paper, and stamps, so I could send away for every booklet and brochure on the topic of health I could find.

During the afternoon, Mom left to buy groceries. The minute she was gone, the phone began to ring. I'd promised her I wouldn't get out of bed, but I was anxious to see how Killion's day went as the new "Ginger." Dragging myself down the hallway, I answered the phone in my best "I've been sick" voice.

"Hello?"

"May I please speak to Emily Crocker?"

It was him! The Mystery Caller!

I suddenly perked up. "Hi! This is Emily Crocker."

"You sound like you know who this is," he teased.

"I do."

"Well then, who is it?"

"Well, I know who you are, but I don't know your name."

"That doesn't make a whole lot of sense, Emily Crocker." He chuckled. "I knew you didn't know my name. I'm Austin Brandt. I can't talk very long because I'm at work. Do you work?" he asked.

"No. I go to school."

"You go to the university, too?"

"No, the high school." I suddenly felt I should apologize for still being in high school. He obviously wasn't. My stomach tightened. He must be a whole lot older than me, I thought, imagining future disapproval from my parents over age.

"So, you're still in high school." It was a statement, not a question, and he sounded disappointed. "Your voice . . . You sounded older."

I quickly changed the subject. "Where do you work?"

"At Pierre's Restaurant. It's a great place to meet girls."

He chuckled, and I wondered why he'd said that to me. He continued. "I'm saving up for an off-campus apartment. Now that I'm nineteen, I'm not required to live in a dorm anymore."

Nineteen, I thought. Why did he have to be so old?

"My old man thinks it'll be a good lesson in responsibility for me to get my own apartment—and pay for it with my own money, too," he added sarcastically, mimicking what I assumed was his father's voice.

We talked for exactly twenty-three-minutes. (I was watching the clock on the living room wall.) I never thought I could ever have a twenty-three-minute conversation with any person of the opposite sex.

But he was so easy to talk to. He told me about his job and the new car his dad, Dr. Brandt, had given him. His boss walked in while we were talking, so he had to hang up. He didn't ask me out, but he *did* ask if he could call again.

He seemed a bit conceited, especially with his frequent comments about other girls. It bothered me a little and I wondered if he were trying to make me feel jealous. But in spite of that, there was something about him that I really did like. It took me a while to figure out exactly what it was. Then it came to me. The whole time we'd talked, he hadn't made one joke—not even a wisecrack! He was "normal," just like me.

I'd barely made it back to bed when Mom came home and the phone rang again. "Emily! Angel's on the phone. Do you feel like talking?"

Do I feel like talking? She must be kidding. I stumbled back down the hallway.

"So, Miss Tarrah, where were you today?"

"Home. Sick. Both my dad and I. How are you feeling?"

"Great! Terrific! Oh, Tarrah, I had the most fantastic day of my whole life. I want to tell you every tiny detail."

"I've got something to tell you, too," I added excitedly.

"Okay, but me first. I can't wait."

I broke in before she could get started. "Hold it. First you've got to tell me what you wore to school today so I can get the whole picture."

"Right. I wore a white sweater so I could use all the rainbow accessories that I bought Saturday. Then I wore my black cords because somewhere in one of those articles I read, it said that black makes you look slimmer. Got it?"

"Got it. Today I wore my teddy bear pajamas, and—"

"Crocker, shut up and listen!"

I leaned against the wall and slid down to the floor, finding a comfortable position as Killion continued. "The morning was pretty much the same as usual. Except I got tons of comments on how I looked."

"Good or bad?"

"Good comments, you idiot." She paused for a minute. "Wait, I left something out. My father was upset when I got home Saturday night because of all the makeup I was wearing. I should have known. So I had to go to school early and put it on there.

"Anyway," she continued, "lunch comes, and I'm sitting alone because you're not there, right? All of a sudden, here comes Danny with Jacob and Sam, and they ask if they can sit with me. I was really surprised. Then Jacob and Sam started teasing me about all the rainbows I was wearing, so Danny told them to knock it off. Wasn't that neat?''

"Yes! Ginger, I think he likes you! Did you notice the way he was staring at you Saturday night?''

"Well, I wasn't really sure. I thought Peter had cut my hair crooked or something . . .'' She paused, chuckling, then continued, "After that, the guys started telling jokes, and they asked me if I knew any. Well, that's like asking Snow White if she knows any dwarfs, right? So I said to them, I'd tell you a joke, but you'd only laugh at me. Well, Crock, they thought that was hilarious. Then I said it was a *Polaroid* joke—it would take them a minute to get the whole picture. That cracked them up! So I went on to tell them this rabbit joke. What would you have if you lined up a whole bunch of rabbits, and they all took one step backward?''

"I don't know. What?''

"A receding hare line!'' She laughed at her own joke. "Crocker, that put them into hysterics. Other people started coming to our table because it looked like we were all having such a great time. Then Danny and I began to joke around just like we always do when we're all over at your house. It was super!''

"Ginger, that sounds really neat.'' I was still waiting for a good place to jump in with my news about the Mystery Caller.

"You know, Tarrah,'' she went on slowly, "usually when I'm around a group of kids at school, I either don't say anything at all, or I try to think of something cool to say. But today I was just myself. I acted the way I always do around you and Kevin, and I didn't feel uncomfortable talking to those guys at all. Isn't that amazing?''

"You think he'll ask you out?''

"Who? Danny? Tarrah, dear, he has a *cat* named Ginger. What if he got us mixed up? Wouldn't that be purr-fect?''

I groaned.

"You've just got to come to school tomorrow, Tarrah.''

"I'll try. I still feel terrible.''

At that instant, Kevin burst noisily into the house.

He pointed at my ear. "That Killion?"

I nodded and he grabbed the phone away from me. "Kill, this is Kevin. Dad told me you talked to him about your diet, and he recommended aerobic exercise. Why don't you come jogging with me in the mornings before school? I run right past your house."

Pulling my robe tighter around me, I waited to get the phone back, wondering how anyone could think of jogging when I felt so miserable.

"Fine. See you in the morning." Kevin hung up the phone. "She had to get off 'cause of her dad." He stepped over me and disappeared down the hall.

I dragged myself back to bed, feeling depressed instead of happy for my best friend. I felt almost jealous that she'd gotten all that attention while I had to stay home all day feeling rotten. I hadn't even gotten to tell her my great news about Austin—the Mystery Caller. But somehow it just didn't seem quite as exciting as her news.

Chapter 7

Normally I enjoy being sick and staying home from school for a few days. Mom always pampers me and I like doing nothing. But when I woke up Tuesday morning and found out Mom had already called the school to tell them I wouldn't be there, I felt really discouraged—even though I also felt really sick.

Bored, I dragged my guitar out of the back of the closet and dusted it off. Kevin and I used to play and sing together, but it'd been a long time. I started picking out some songs I remembered, and pretty soon Dad wandered into my room. We had our own sing-along. It was fun, but Wendy kept trying to join in from the other room so we stopped.

Dad retired the guitar back into my closet. I wondered if I looked as pale as he did. "You have a terrific voice, Hon. You should be in the choir at school."

I shrugged. I'd managed to avoid joining clubs because they always seemed to be having swim parties or horseback rides. I didn't want to be embarrassed by not knowing how to do anything. Besides, I wouldn't want to join a club without Killion. We always did everything together, but her singing ability rated right up there with my cooking ability.

I spent most of the afternoon feeling sorry for myself, and imagining Killion at school, having all kinds of fun. There were probably ninety-five guys sitting with her at lunch, laughing at her jokes, and fighting over who was going to walk her to each class. Even Kevin, my own brother, had asked her to go jogging. Did they invite *me* to come along? No way.

I climbed out of bed to straighten up the clothes I'd laid out two nights ago and still hadn't had a chance to wear. On Saturday I'd had this wonderful, new feeling. I thought I looked good for the first time in my life, and I thought that feeling of confidence would stick with me throughout the school week.

Imagine me, posing like a model out on a public street for whoever was passing by. I'd never done anything crazy like that before, and the way I felt right now, I'd probably never act that freely in public again. All that confidence was gone, and I was back to the same old gloomy me.

I put the record "At Seventeen" on the stereo, leaving the arm up so it would keep playing:

> "The valentines I never knew
> The Friday night charades of youth
> were spent on one more beautiful
> At seventeen, I learned the truth. . . ."

Settling back down under the covers, I propped up a mirror and applied more medication to my face. It burned and itched a little, turning my skin red. I hoped I could cover it with makeup when I went back to school. Glancing at my beautiful new hair style, I winced. It was now flat and matted down with a few hairs sticking up in the wrong direction. Welcome back to the real world, Crocker, I thought.

Dad came in to check me over. Sometimes it's nice to have a doctor for a father—and sometimes it's not. After much arguing, he convinced me I needed to stay home another day.

"But you're going back to work tomorrow," I pleaded, "and we had the same illness."

"Yes, Hon," he agreed as he studied the thermometer, tugging at his beard, "but I weigh twice as much as you and it was easier for me to get my strength back. Mom says you've hardly eaten a thing." He looked at me sternly.

"You're not going on a diet just because Angel is, are you?"

"No, Dad. Sometimes I just don't feel like eating much."

He tousled my hair. "Sounds like you're having growing pains. Anything you want to talk about?"

I shook my head no, and gave him a hug. I was glad he felt concerned, but parents are parents and you just can't tell them all your problems like you can a good friend.

Mom appeared at the door. "There's a boy on the phone who wants to talk to you, Em." She had a curious look on her face.

"See?" Dad grinned at me. "Growing up isn't all bad."

It was Austin again! Two days in a row he'd called. Before I knew it, a half hour had flown by as we talked and laughed. Then suddenly I realized why it was so easy to talk to him—he did all the talking, and I did all the listening. It bothered me a little. There were things I would've liked to talk to him about, too. But I'd never had a guy call me before—just to talk—so maybe that's the way it was.

Mom respected my privacy and kept her distance at first, but then she started dropping hints.

"Em, you'll get sick all over again if you tire yourself out!" she called. Then, "There's a draft through the hallway. You'd better get back into bed!"

"Austin, I have to hang up now."

"Wait a second," he said. "I'd really like to meet you in person, Emily. I want to ask you out, but I never know whether or not I have to work on weekends until the last minute. If we make plans for Saturday night and I have to cancel, will you understand?"

"Sure, Austin." Ninety-five thoughts were flashing through my head all at once. Slow down, I thought. I'm not ready for this yet. I searched frantically for a way out. Suddenly I didn't want him to ask me for a date. But hadn't I been dying for him to do just that? I was really confused.

He continued, "I've been wanting to see that new movie *Nightingale*. Will you go with me Saturday?"

"Um, Austin." I stalled him, trying to think quickly while explaining to him why I'd been home all week. "Can you call back later?" The last thing I wanted to say was I had to ask my parents for permission first, and it was going to take a lot of convincing since I really didn't even know him. He'd certainly think I was too young then.

"Sure," he agreed to my plan. "You don't have a serious illness, I hope."

"Emily!" Mom sounded irritated.

"No, I'll live. Bye, Austin." Reluctantly hanging up the phone, I hurried back to my room.

"Is that a boy from school, dear?"

I quickly stuck the thermometer into my mouth, so I didn't have to answer. "Mmmmmmmm!" I called back to her.

Chapter 8

The second Kevin got home from school, I ordered him into my room. "Sit down and shut the door."

He looked at me strangely. "Don't you mean shut the door and then sit down?"

"Whatever," I muttered as I waved my hand at him. "Kevin, I've got a problem, and I need your advice."

He sat down on the edge of the bed. "I'll only listen if you stop playing that stupid record!" He leaned over and clicked off my stereo.

"Sorry. All right, listen carefully. I met this terrific guy."

"That's a problem?"

"Just listen. I met this terrific guy, but I haven't *really* met him yet."

He looked puzzled.

"You see, I've only talked to him on the phone."

"Oh. Who set you up?"

"Nobody. It was a wrong number."

His face slowly broke into a grin as he realized what I was telling him. "You mean you dialed a wrong number, this guy answered, and you fell in love?"

"No. You've got it backwards. *He* dialed wrong. He was calling another girl, and he got me instead."

"Oh, that's even better. Calling another girl, huh?"

"There's more," I continued, absently folding down the bedspread. "He's nineteen, he's got a job, he's looking for an apartment, and he asked me out to see *Nightingale* on Saturday night." I leaned against the pillow and crossed my arms. "There, what do you think?"

"I think you left out one problem."

"What?"

"That movie is rated R. You're not old enough to see it."

Sliding down, I pulled the covers over my head. "What else?" I mumbled.

"Look, Em, the real problem is this: Mom and Dad aren't going to let you go out with a guy you met over the phone accidentally, and they'll think he's too old for you. You're not allowed to see R-rated movies, and if I were you, I wouldn't even *mention* the part about getting his own apartment."

I sat up. "Oh, Kevin, what should I do? He's the first guy I've ever met—*almost* met—that I can talk to. I really like him."

"What if he turns out to be a jerk?"

"He's *not* a jerk. I know his personality."

"What if he *looks* like a jerk?"

I hesitated. "I thought about that. But I'm more worried that he's gonna be real sorry when *he* sees *me*. . . ."

"Hey, come on, Em. Don't put yourself down. This guy will be lucky if he's ever seen out on a date with you—he just doesn't know it yet."

"Thanks, Kev." I got a lump in my throat. He'd never complimented me before. But I still wasn't convinced.

"Hey," he went on, "who is this guy anyway? Has he ever tried anything with my little sister?"

"You can't kiss over the telephone, idiot."

Kevin did his best Groucho Marx imitation. "You can if you're both in the same telephone booth."

He finally succeeded in making me laugh.

"Okay," he continued, "let's get serious. I've got a plan."

"Shoot."

"To get out of going to the movie, you tell him you've been sick all week, which is true, and you invite him over here Saturday night for . . ." He paused. "Well, I was going to say that you could bake him something for dessert, but you don't want to kill him. At least not on the first date."

I threw a pillow at him.

"Okay," he went on, "big brother solves problem number one. Now, I wouldn't worry about his age. Who's going to know?"

"Mom and Dad, that's who."

"Naw. Chances are, they won't ask. If they do—just say you don't know."

"Kevin, I can't lie. You know that. It's one of my biggest faults."

He rolled his eyes, then paused, thinking. "Hey, Em, remember when Mom showed us the diary she'd kept when she was your age?"

I nodded.

"And she read us what she'd written on the day she met Dad?"

I nodded again.

"She described what he looked like and how old he was."

I sat up straight. "He was nineteen!" I exclaimed, remembering. "And Mom was only fifteen. It's the same age difference as Austin and me."

"That's right," Kevin said. "File that information away and use it when you need it."

"Kevin, you're brilliant."

"I know," he agreed. "Okay, that's settled. Next, you tell Mom and Dad it's a blind date, which it sort of is, right? So this way, he comes over, and you can check each other out. If he turns out to be Mr. Teenage Ugly of America, you don't have to spend an embarrassing evening out in public with him."

"And what if he thinks that I'm *Miss* Teenage Ugly of America?"

Kevin got up and did his macho imitation for me. "Hey, would a hunk like me have a sister who was ugly? No way!"

Two compliments in one day, I thought. What a surprise. "You know," I said slowly, hugging my knees to my chest, "it might work."

"Of course it'll work." He grinned, saluted me, and slipped out the door.

I leaned back against a pillow and repeated to myself, it just might work. . . .

Chapter 9

Wednesday was terrible. A little bit of rest and recovery goes a long way when you're trying to encourage a social life to develop.

I couldn't get Austin off my mind. I had three days to get ready for our date on Saturday and to somehow explain him to Mom and Dad. The more I thought about Kevin's plan, the better I liked it. My parents shouldn't object to my inviting someone over to the house. They would be in the family room, which meant Austin and I could be alone in the kitchen.

But I was so nervous. I had a knot in my stomach, and every time I thought about meeting Austin, the knot grew bigger. I didn't feel like eating at all, so I wasn't surprised to discover that I'd lost five pounds since I'd gotten sick. I was losing ground on my goal to gain weight.

To make matters worse, I kept thinking about Rene—or Renee, or Renée—the girl Austin had been calling when he'd gotten me instead. Who was she? A girlfriend? I was afraid to ask him because I really didn't want to hear about another girl he might be dating. I toyed with the idea of casually mentioning her if he called today, but he hadn't so far. Of course I couldn't expect him to call every day, but I hated the feeling of waiting for the phone to ring, practically jumping out of my skin every time it did, then being disappointed when it wasn't for me.

Killion's phone call last night had depressed me even further. She'd gone on and on about how she'd been the center of attention at lunch again, sitting with Danny, Jacob, and Sam. Sam had even walked her part of the way home after school. I wondered if she ever wanted me to eat lunch with her again. I might get in the way of her new fan club. Oh, what a rotten thing to think about my best friend. And I still hadn't even told her about Austin yet.

I couldn't help remembering the story Killion had told me about Loni Ames. Loni's parents had given her a phone of her own for a birthday present, but she was getting so many calls from guys she knew and guys she didn't know, her parents made her get a new number which was unlisted.

Imagine, Killion had said, being so popular that you were the girl with the unlisted number. And here I am, I thought, lying in bed for three days in a row, knowing that no one at school probably even noticed I was missing. Loni may have an unlisted phone number, but I've got an unlisted life. Hey, I like that, I thought. The girl with the unlisted life. That's me.

Getting out of bed, I tiptoed into the nursery to check on Wendy for the umpteenth time. Mom had gone out and left me in charge, Dad had returned to work, so Wendy and I were alone.

I leaned over the bassinet to watch her as she slept. She seemed so tiny and helpless, curled up in a little ball. All she cared about was getting food and attention whenever she wanted it. A full tummy and a warm bed were all she needed. When was it that life started getting so complicated?

I tiptoed out again, hoping she'd stay asleep until Mom got home so I wouldn't have to deal with tears or dirty diapers.

I wondered if Killion was home from school yet but decided not to tie up the phone—just in case. I got out my guitar instead, playing and singing softly so I wouldn't disturb Wendy. I'd managed to pick out the chords to the song "At Seventeen," and I actually thought I sounded pretty good. I tried to put as much sorrow into my voice as Janis Ian did.

Suddenly the phone rang, and my heart jumped up and stuck in my throat. I raced down the hall, then stopped to let it ring one extra time, so I wouldn't seem too anxious.

"Hello?" I said in a voice that sounded like my heart was stuck in my throat.

"Tarrah!" Killion cried from the other end. She'd been overdoing the enthusiasm bit all week. "How are you feeling today?"

"If you really want to know, I'm bored to death, and I haven't been eating or sleeping. I even left the radio on all night."

"You did? How'd it fit?"

"Oh, Ginger, I've missed you so much," I confessed, feeling guilty about the thoughts that had been going through my mind earlier. "I've even missed your terrible jokes, although I never thought I'd say that."

"I've missed you too, Tarrah, and I've just *got* to tell you about today before I die! I didn't know that getting that make-over last weekend was going to change my life so drastically."

"It didn't."

"What do you mean—it didn't?"

"Oh, Killion—I mean, Ginger. It wasn't your make-over that did anything. Think about it. You just started your diet this week, so you can't attribute any of this recent popularity to that. Your new glasses haven't even come in yet, so it's not that either."

"Well, what is it then?"

"You told me yourself on Monday. You started being the crazy person that you are with Kevin and me around the other kids at school. It happened this week because I wasn't around, taking up all your time and attention as usual, so you had to relate to other people."

I paused for emphasis. "Don't you see? You're just letting the personality that was always there shine through, without being afraid of what someone's going to think of you."

"Heavy."

"No it's not—it's simple. And you just happened to be in the right place at the right time."

"You're right, Crocker—I mean, Tarrah." She considered it for a few moments. "I'm going to give that some more thought later, but right now I've got to tell you what happened today. . . ."

"No way!" I interrupted. "It's *me* first this time, before your dad makes you hang up. Guess who called me?"

"Who? Oh, wait, I think I know. The Mystery Caller?"

"Yes!"

"He did? When?"

"Monday and Tuesday."

"Why didn't you tell me before?"

"I've been trying to tell you, but I haven't been able to get a word in edgewise, as my dad would say."

"Oh, Crocker, I'm really sorry."

Killion listened as I told her all about Austin.

"That's fantastic!" She hesitated, then lowered her voice as if someone could hear our conversation. "Did you say he was nineteen?"

"Yes." I groaned. "That's the worst part. And get this—he's looking for an apartment."

"Does he know which way it went?"

I ignored that and continued, "Killion, I'm a nervous wreck. I'm dying for the weekend to come, and at the same time, I don't want it to come." Without realizing it, I'd twisted the phone cord into a tangled knot.

"I'm so excited for you," she said.

"I'm not. I almost wish the whole thing hadn't happened. I was so secure knowing that I'd always be home alone every Saturday night for the rest of my life, and now this comes along and changes everything."

"Don't be silly, Tarrah. Do you really want to spend another Saturday night at home? Besides, don't you want to be able to compare notes about our first dates?"

"You're kidding!" I exclaimed. "Danny asked you out?"

"No. Jacob did."

"Jacob? The rich guy?"

"Rich? His family's got so much money, Crock, you wouldn't believe it! I went through the lunch line with him today, and when we got to the cash register, he pulled out bills with pictures of presidents on them I'd never even heard of before."

"But I thought Danny . . ."

"So did I," she interrupted. "And even Sam had hinted that we ought to go over to MacKenzie's some night. So I was really surprised when Jacob asked me."

"That's great. What'd your dad say?"

"Ha, you have to ruin everything, don't you? He'll probably say I can't date until I'm thirty." She sighed. "I haven't told him yet, but I figure that since Jacob is such a good, strong name from the Bible, he might be swayed."

"So's Danny."

"So's Danny what?"

"His name. It's from the Bible, too. Daniel."

"Oh, I never thought of that. Well, come to think of it, Sam may be short for Samuel, or even Samson. Maybe our upstanding Reverend Killion will approve of all three of them!"

"Let's see," I added, thinking. "Angel is definitely in the Bible, too, but what about Emily?"

"I don't know. I'd have to check."

"Oh, well, at least it's in the phone book. I know that's not quite the same as being in the Bible, but it's just about as useful to me."

Chapter 10

"I forgot to tell you something last night," Killion announced early the next morning as we walked to school. "There's a new girl who just moved here, and she's in my gym class. Believe it or not, she's already hooked up with Loni and Stacy. You'll know why when you see her. Seems to me there ought to be some kind of rule about not being able to transfer into a new school if you're gorgeous. Oh, and get this, her name is Bitsy. Bitsy McGee. Do you believe that? Talk about cute names! Her mother must have had a cute *attack* right after Bitsy was born to come up with a name like that. And besides all that, she shows up every day wearing a fresh flower in her hair. Incredible!"

I was trying to be attentive, but I couldn't get my thoughts off myself. Today would be the first day that the "new me" would be seen in school, and I was feeling extremely self-conscious. I finally had the chance to wear all the clothes and accessories that I'd laid out four days ago, only to find that they didn't fit as well as they had when I weighed more.

I'd gotten up earlier than usual and spent a long time on my hair to get it just right. Actually, I felt self-conscious because I thought I looked good, except for one thing—my face. I knew the redness and peeling were signs that the medication was working, but I wished I could have rented someone else's face for a few weeks while mine healed— like Killion's "Angel face." Even better than that, I thought, would be to borrow Wendy's perfect skin. Flawless skin should last longer than the first ten years of our life, shouldn't it? I laughed at the thought.

"What are you laughing about?"

"Oh, Ginger." I sighed as I adjusted one of my accessories—the scarf which was fashionably knotted around my neck. "I'm just a little nervous today. No one has seen me as a blond yet, remember?"

During the morning I got several comments about my appearance—mostly from teachers, unfortunately. But I did get more smiles and stares than usual, plus a few double takes. I ran into Danny and Kevin on my way to lunch and they hollered and whistled, embarrassing me to death.

I met Killion and we sat at our usual table. Within minutes, we were surrounded by her new fan club—Jacob, Sam, Danny, and even Kevin today.

"Killion," I whispered to her, "I'll eat somewhere else today if you want to sit alone with . . . uh . . . the guys."

"What? Don't be silly, Crocker. You're my best friend."

That made me feel a little better, but once again, I felt nervous trying to eat while surrounded by guys. I ended up hardly eating anything and worrying that if the guys started eating with us every day, by June I'd be invisible.

I was honestly proud of the way Killion had been sticking to her diet. She'd already lost three pounds in less than a week. As I tried to choke down my sandwich, she laid three pills on the table, then glanced at me. "Your dad tried to talk me out of taking diet pills. He said you have to be real careful with some of them, and made me promise to take them for only two weeks."

I looked at the three capsules. "What's the red pill?"

"I take that before lunch."

"What's the blue pill?"

"I take that after lunch."

Then the whole table asked in unison, "What's the yellow pill?"

"That's lunch. . . ."

The guys cracked up, a little too loudly, I thought. That started off the wisecracking, which really made me feel left out as usual. I never could compete around Kevin and Killion as it was, much less with three others jumping in with the jokes.

The laughter got louder as the jokes got worse. Suddenly Kevin leaned over behind Danny's back and grabbed my arm. "You okay, Em?"

"Yeah. I guess I'm just a little out of it from being away for so long. Sorry if I'm spoiling the party."

"You're not. Are you sure nothing else is bothering you? Like maybe, a certain wrong number?" He winked his eye several times.

"Sure, I guess that's part of it. I'll be fine, Kev. Thanks for asking."

I excused myself to dump my lunch tray and no one even noticed I was leaving. They were all laughing at Killion's last joke.

I hurried down the hall, wanting some extra time to comb my hair before next period because I was feeling a little nervous about English class with Michael Farrah. I was afraid he'd notice me and I was afraid he wouldn't.

In the girls' room, Stacy Benson stood next to me, patting her perfect hair as we primped together in front of the mirror. Comparing our reflections gave me second thoughts about how good I thought I looked. I stayed behind for a few moments after she left, wondering if there was anything more I could do to improve the image staring back at me. I decided I didn't have time for major plastic surgery before English, so I gave up and hustled to class, trying to run without messing up my hair.

Flying around the corner to the door of the classroom, I plowed straight into Michael Farrah. He caught me by the shoulders as I started to lose my balance.

"I—I'm sorry," I apologized.

"That's okay, Emily. I shouldn't have been blocking the doorway." He kept hold of me as his incredibly blue eyes looked me up and down, then gazed into mine.

"Have you been out?"

HE'D NOTICED! Feeling embarrassed by all the eye contact, I dropped my eyes. "Well, I've been sick at home all week," I answered bashfully. How do you make being sick sound interesting?

He smiled and gave my shoulders a little squeeze before letting go. My heart was beating about ninety-five times a second. Very slowly he replied, "You sure don't look like you've been sick to me. . . ."

The bell rang as I floated to my seat and settled into a good position to stare at the back of his neck. The ecstatically high feeling he'd just given me didn't last for long, though. As a matter of fact, it instantly plummeted as a bouncy little blond, dressed in a white lace, old-fashioned style dress, with a white orchid in her hair, bounced through the door, bounced across the room, and bounced into the desk right in front of Michael Farrah. She turned sideways in her chair and smiled back at him.

A low voice from the back of the room whispered mockingly, "Those two gettin' married today?" Another voice answered, "They must be. She looks like she just fell off the top of a wedding cake."

I didn't like the way she was smiling at *my* Michael Farrah.

"You're late, Bitsy!" Ms. Milliren's voice made me jump.

Bitsy. My mind flashed back to my conversation with Killion. So that's Bitsy McGee. Why does she have to sit right in front of Michael Farrah? I thought about Loni Ames' advice—pick out the best-looking guy in the room and sit right in front of him if you want to get noticed. Why did other girls have all the nerve I lacked?

After class I tried to time my exit so I'd run into him again at the door, but he stayed behind to re-explain the assignment to Bitsy. I wondered why fate couldn't have let me enjoy my one moment of social success longer than a mere ten seconds before shooting me down.

"So, how was your first day as the new and exciting Emily 'Tarrah' Crocker?" Killion asked on the way home.

I was dragging my feet, exhausted by my return to the outside world. "Not nearly as exciting as your first day as the new Angel 'Ginger' Killion." Maybe it was my imagination but I thought she looked pleased. "Let me ask you something," I said to her slowly. "If a guy tells you that you don't look sick to him, can you take that as a compliment?"

She laughed. "You're really digging, Crocker. Who said that to you—Michael Farrah?"

"Yes."

"You're kidding!" She stared at me, then turned the other way. "Um, did I tell you that Jacob is already planning a big party at his house for Christmas and we're all invited?"

"You don't have to change the subject, Kill. I saw Michael Farrah and Bitsy McGee together today. Has that been developing all week?"

"Yep. Ever since she bounced in the front door for the first time." She squeezed my arm. "I'm sorry, Crock."

I headed across the street, dodging a car I hadn't seen. "That's okay," I snapped. "Who needs Michael Farrah, anyway? I've got my very own Mystery Caller." I stopped to twirl around in the middle of the street. "And besides," I continued, acting normal again as I hopped up on the sidewalk, "I think it's going to take more than a new hair style to interest Mr. Farrah. Is there an operation that makes you bouncy?"

"How about trying a new shade of lip gloss?" she teased.

"That's it! I'll switch from mopey mauve to look-at-me-lavender. I'll have them lining up at my locker to carry my books!" I slapped her on the back. "You're a genius, Ginger. Have you got any *plants* I can stick in my hair?"

At least laughing with Killion made the hurt and disappointment that gnawed at my insides disappear for a few minutes. How come she had made such a big splash at school after her make-over and I'd made barely a ripple?

The fairy tale of the ugly duckling flashed through my mind. Hadn't we both gone through the metamorphosis? How could one ugly duckling turn into a swan while the other one remained the same? Would my first date with Austin be as big a flop as my first day back at school?

Arriving home. I rushed down the hall to the safety of my room, where I could shut out the world and avoid questions. I put my record on the stereo and fell onto the bed in a heap, closing my eyes to block the flow of tears I felt rising as I listened to my song:

"It was long ago and far away
The world was younger than today
and dreams were all they gave for free
to ugly duckling girls like me. . . ."

Chapter II

On Saturday morning, Kevin talked me into jogging with him and Killion. I didn't have a fancy jogging outfit to wear, so I just wore some faded blue jeans, old tennis shoes, and an ancient flannel shirt of Kevin's which was about ninety-five sizes too big for me. I didn't bother to fix my hair or put on any makeup. My skin was still peeling from the medication, so I decided to leave it bare until Saturday night and hope for the best.

Austin had never called back. I wondered if he'd forgotten about our date for tonight. Sooner or later, I was going to have to mention it to my parents. I figured they'd give me the third degree, and I didn't want to have to break up with the guy before I'd even met him.

"Emily!" Mom called as we were heading out the door. "You shouldn't go out and run in this cold weather after being sick."

"Don't worry, Mom. Jogging is healthy. Kevin says it makes you hungry, so I'll probably come home and eat ninety-five pancakes for breakfast."

"Well, all right. But don't overdo it." She kissed me on the cheek. "And here," she added, pulling an old ski cap over my hair, "you shouldn't go out without something on your head."

I laughed at my ridiculous reflection in the mirror. "I couldn't look any worse if I tried!" Haphazardly I stuffed the ends of my hair up under the ski cap.

Kevin started yelling at me from the front yard. "Come on, Rocky, I'm ready to start your training!" He danced around like a boxer until I joined him. "First, you gotta

46

stretch out your muscles so you don't pull any. Watch.''
He did a few bends and twists, then put one foot at a time
up against a tree to stretch out his leg muscles. I followed
his lead.

"Okay, here we go!" he hollered as he took off. We
ran across one street and down another. "You're going to
feel tired at first, but try not to think about it. Eventually
you'll get a second wind so you can keep going.''

He said no more as we jogged over to Killion's house. I
matched his pace and felt terrible right away, just like he
said I would.

Killion was waiting and joined us as we passed by. It
was too hard to talk and run at the same time, so we didn't
talk. I could tell she was excited about her date with Jacob
for tonight. She'd been so hyper all week. I didn't know if
it was because of Jacob or the diet pills. I shook my head
''no'' in response to her impression of answering a telephone. I assumed she was asking me if Austin had called.

After about twenty minutes, I'd had all I could take of
the wonderful world of jogging. I waved good-bye to
Killion and Kevin, and headed back home alone.

As I was coming down the home stretch, I noticed a
strange car parked in front of my house. There was a guy
sitting in the front seat, but I didn't think it was Danny. I
cut across the yard and headed for the front door. The guy
got out of the car and waved at me.

"Emily Crocker?"

I stopped and stared at him. "Yes?"

"Hi, Emily. I'm Austin Brandt.''

If I could have pushed a button and disappeared into
hyperspace at that instant, I would have. I imagined how I
must have looked, standing there with that ski cap pulled
down to my eyebrows, no makeup, and Kevin's baggy
shirt on. I took a few steps toward the car, then stopped.
The thought flashed through my mind that the further away
I was, the better I might look.

"Austin. Hi.'' I waved back weakly. I couldn't think of
a single thing to say. My heart was turning cartwheels
inside of my chest.

"I just got called into work for the rest of the night, so

there goes our date. But I did want to stop by and officially meet you in person.''

He hesitated. "It's easier to dream about a girl when you know what she looks like." He laughed. "Come closer. I don't bite." He laughed again. "I just had a nice conversation with your mother. She told me you were out jogging and that I should wait for you."

Thanks a lot, Mom, I thought. How could you do this to me? I started walking toward him slowly. "Austin, I—I wish you'd called first." I tore the ski cap off and tried to fluff up my flat hair. Then, on second thought, I pulled it back on again. "Look at me. I've got these old clothes on, and my hair . . . Oh, Austin, I hope first impressions don't count with you, because I don't really look like this."

I stopped in front of him. Kevin was definitely wrong. Austin didn't look like a jerk at all. He was gorgeous, with light brown hair almost as long as mine. He had a mustache and the greenest eyes I'd ever seen.

He leaned against the car, crossed his arms, and smirked at me. He must have thought it was funny to see me standing there, embarrassed and apologizing for the way I looked.

"Are you laughing at me?" I tried to stuff the long shirttail back into my jeans. All of a sudden, I felt like I really didn't know this person. I just couldn't connect the voice on the phone to his face or mannerisms.

He took hold of my arm and pulled me closer. "No, I'm not laughing at you. I think you look kinda cute. Like a real jogger."

"A jogger who can't afford a real jogging outfit." Why was I apologizing? "So, tonight is off." I tried to sound matter-of-fact, feeling disappointed and relieved at the same time. I didn't think it was necessary to tell him I'd changed the plans anyway.

"Yeah, I'm sorry. How about trying it again next Friday?"

I finally smiled at him, forgetting to hide my braces. "Are you sure?" I wished I could stop my knees from shaking.

"Sure I'm sure. Do you think you could find something a little dressier to wear?"

I assumed he was teasing, since he hadn't stopped smirking at me. "Of course," I answered, wondering how bad my peeling skin looked in the sunlight. "And Austin? I promise that when you come back next Friday, you'll see a completely different girl."

That hopeful comment got no response other than a glance at his watch. "Better go or I'll be late for work." He reached out and shook my hand. "Nice to meet you, Emily Crocker."

The pleasure was all mine, I thought as I watched him race his car off down the street, screeching his tires. I hoped Mom hadn't heard it.

Kevin jogged up at the same moment. He leaned over, putting his hands on his knees, and gasped for air. "Who's that?" he huffed.

"Guess."

"You're kidding! That was your wrong number?"

"Yes." I sighed. "He had to cancel our date for tonight. At least that solves about ninety-five of my problems right there." I ripped off the ski cap and hurled it across the front yard. "Kevin, look at me! He's probably thinking that he's made a colossal mistake. Do you think first impressions count?"

"Were you impressed with him?"

"YES!"

"Did he ask you out again?"

"Yeah, but he probably felt obligated."

"Don't worry, Sis." Kevin put his arm around my shoulders and steered me toward the front door. "Don't you believe in love at second sight?"

As I expected, I was put on trial the minute I walked through the front door.

"Would you mind explaining who that young man was?" Mom asked, sounding angry. I noticed that Dad was trying hard not to smile as he sipped his coffee. He avoided my eyes.

"Um, he's a friend of mine." I tried to collect my

thoughts. "He's the guy who's been calling me on the phone."

She raised her voice. "He said something about your date for tonight. Emily, did you think you were going out on a date—with a boy in a car—without asking your father and me for permission to go?"

"No, Mom, I . . ."

"When did he ask you?"

"On Tuesday, but . . ."

"Tuesday? That was four days ago. Why didn't you mention it earlier?"

"Mom, give me a chance to explain. I was going to tell you about it as soon as our plans were definite. He has to work tonight, so now we're not going anywhere at all."

Her frown disappeared. "All right, Em. But I had no idea who he was or what he was talking about."

"I'm sorry, Mom. I should have told you sooner." I hesitated, wondering if I should just drop the whole thing. I decided to ask anyway. "Can we go out next Friday?"

She exchanged glances with my dad. "Emily, why have we never heard of him before? We usually know who your friends are. Is he new at school?"

"No. He . . . uh . . ."

"What's his name?"

"Austin Brandt."

"Brandt?" Dad repeated, scratching his beard. "Of course, Austin Brandt." He turned toward Mom. "Dear, that's Dr. Brandt's son. We make our rounds at the hospital at the same time. As a matter of fact, I've met Austin before—several times. I should have answered the door. I'm sure I would have recognized him. He's a nice young man."

Mom brushed the hair back from my forehead with her hand. "Well, in that case, I guess it's all right. But from now on, Em, let's not keep secrets."

"Okay, Mom." I couldn't resist grabbing my dad and giving him a big hug. "Thanks for sticking up for me," I whispered to him.

As I passed Kevin on the way to my room, I heard him mumble in a low voice, "Talk about being lucky . . . ."

Chapter 12

Mom always cooked up a big breakfast on Sunday morning. It was a Crocker family tradition. However, *this* Sunday morning, I'd found a recipe in my beginner's cookbook called Easy Eggs. The "easy" part was debatable, but with Mom's help I served up a breakfast that had Dad and Kevin asking for seconds. I felt a real sense of accomplishment.

After we ate, Mom disappeared to nurse Wendy while the rest of us cleaned the kitchen. Dad handed me plates as I loaded the dishwasher. "Are you getting caught up on your school work after being sick?" he asked.

"I'm trying. The biggest problem is English. We have to do a research paper, then give a speech in front of the class. I hate to give speeches. I get so nervous before it's my turn that my mouth feels like sandpaper."

"Hon, everyone feels the same. Think of it that way. Even teachers get nervous the first time they have to face a new class."

"I know. But I'm the only one in the room who wears braces, and, I know this sounds silly, but sometimes when I'm talking, my lip gets caught on the wires and I have to reach up and unhook it. What if that happens in the middle of my speech? I'd die!"

Kevin had been trying not to laugh, but he finally gave in to it. "You have more problems than a math book!" He threw a sponge at me. "What's your speech going to be about?"

"That's another thing. The topic has to have something to do with our town. I haven't been able to come up with a good idea yet." I thought for a moment. "Dad, were any famous men or women ever born here?"

"No, Hon. The only people born here have all been little babies."

I groaned. "I guess I'll have to hit the library."

"And hope that inspiration hits you back," he added.

"What about all those library books in your room?" Kevin asked. "It looks like you've been doing research already."

"Oh, those are mostly on health and diets. Mmmmm," I thought out loud. "Wait a minute. Is there any way I can relate that topic to this town? My research would be nearly finished already if I could. . . ."

Dad leaned against the refrigerator and stroked his beard as he considered the idea. "You know, Hon, we have a walk-in health clinic at the hospital. They treat minor ailments and injuries. Plus, they dispense health care information about diets, nutrition, and exercise. It's kind of a service to the public. They even use volunteer help, if you're interested."

I *was* interested—very. "That sounds great, Dad. Forget the research paper and speech, I'd be interested anyway."

"As a matter of fact," he continued, "I think you know someone who works there—Jenny Killion, Angel's cousin."

"That's right! I knew she worked at the hospital, but I didn't know what she did."

"You could check it out this afternoon if you want to ride to the hospital with me."

"Great idea, Dad."

For the rest of the morning, I wandered around the house, unable to concentrate on anything but Austin and the sore muscles that jogging had left me. It hurt every time I moved, but I decided to go for a walk anyway, taking Kevin's advice that using my leg muscles would help work the soreness out.

The autumn sun felt warm on my face, and a cool breeze tickled through my hair. I'd taken time to shower and dress nicely, just in case I happened to run into anyone again.

I had a sense of calmness inside of me after spending another miserable Saturday night home alone. It made it worse to know that Killion was out on a date with Jacob, but I actually felt relieved that I hadn't gone out with Austin. Now I could relax for a few days and still have time to get nervous all over again for Friday night.

Making a loop around the block, I returned home just as Mom, Dad, and Wendy were leaving to go shopping. I waved them off and opened the front door to the sound of a ringing telephone. I lunged for it, only to hear a click as the person on the other end hung up.

"Kevin!" I shouted angrily. "Why didn't you answer the phone?"

He appeared in the hallway, wearing a bath towel, his wet hair sticking up in all directions. "I was in the shower."

"I've gotten out of the shower to answer the phone for you!" I snapped.

He looked at me strangely. "Hey, calm down, Em. I'm sorry. I had soap in my eyes and I didn't see the phone ringing."

"Oh, Kevin." I flopped down on the couch. "Why am I being so nasty to you?"

"That's what I'm supposed to say."

I punched out one of the sofa pillows.

"Say," he continued, "Danny's picking me up in a few minutes and we're going to check out a car that's for sale. We can drop you off at the clinic on our way if you'd like."

"That'd be great, Kev. I'll leave Dad a note."

He disappeared down the hall to get dressed.

"Can I fix you some lunch?" I called after him, feeling a sudden new sense of confidence in my cooking ability.

"No thanks. We're just going to drop you off. I don't have time to stay and have my stomach pumped. . . ."

When I arrived at the clinic, Jenny Killion gave me the grand tour, then put me to work doing something easy: signing in patients and keeping track of who was where. Sunday afternoons were fairly slow, she explained, so I'd have time to observe a lot of what was going on.

Jenny resembled Killion in many ways. She had the

same big, brown eyes, pretty skin, and the same problem of gaining weight too easily. She was a dietician and worked with patients at the hospital who'd been assigned special diets or exercise programs.

Around two o'clock, the clinic emptied and I was able to slip into the back and browse around. I helped myself to some free literature I found on health and exercise. As I was leaning over a glass case which displayed different types of medical instruments, a young guy walked in carrying supplies. He wore a white volunteer's jacket like the one I had on. His hair was the color mine had been before it was "sun-painted," and he was tall—really tall. He seemed to be all arms and legs.

"Hi." He greeted me, awkwardly pushing up his glasses with his knuckle while juggling boxes in one arm. "You must be Jenny's cousin, Angel."

"Hi. No, I'm Jenny's cousin's friend." He has nice eyes, I thought. "I'm Emily Crocker." I was starting to get a crick in my neck from staring up at him.

"I'm Mark Logan. Are you going to be working here as a volunteer?" He looked worried, as if the fate of the world depended on my answer.

I shrugged my shoulders. "I'm not sure." Hesitating, I glanced around, noting the supplies Mark had stockpiled in preparation for the next rush of patients, and I knew right away I wanted to be a part of it. "You know, Mark—" I looked up at him again "—I think I'm gonna do it!" I couldn't help noticing his eyes again. They were bluer than Michael Farrah's.

"Great!" His worried look melted into a smile. He had braces on his teeth! I was really surprised, so I smiled back at him.

"Hey, we have something in common." He chuckled. "We're both behind bars!" We laughed at our shared misfortune.

"I should get back to the receptionist's desk." I waved and headed toward the door. "See you later, Mark."

"I hope so." When he turned to set the boxes down, they slipped from his hands and crashed to the floor. I saw it all out of the corner of my eye. He rolled his eyes at me, looking embarrassed. "Mr. Macho strikes again," he muttered as he began picking things up.

The clinic was fascinating to me. I even got a chance to "interview" Jenny as part of my research so I could learn more about her job. She invited me to go to an exercise-dance class with her which she taught twice a week. The exercises were aerobic dances to popular music.

It sounded great, much better than jogging, I thought as I again became aware of the soreness I felt. Jenny signed me up to work at the clinic on Tuesdays and Thursdays so I could go to the class with her afterwards.

The rest of the day flew by, and I was surprised when I looked up and saw Kevin and Danny waiting for me. I leaned through the doorway to holler good-bye to Jenny.

Through the half-opened door I could see Mark staring out at Kevin and Danny with a sad look on his face. "Bye, Mark," I called.

He turned his attention to me. "Bye, Angel."

"No, it's Emily," I corrected him. "Angel is Jenny's cousin." As I turned to leave, I distinctly heard him say softly, "You sure look like an Angel to me. . . ."

Chapter 13

Kevin and Danny each grabbed one of my elbows and escorted me out to the parking lot, saying what a big surprise they had in store for me.

"Ta-dah!" Kevin threw his arms out over a piece of red metal with four wheels. I guessed it was a car. One dent ran into another. There wasn't a smooth spot anywhere on the surface.

The inside was just as bad, I noticed as I snagged my hose on the ripped upholstery. I thought I was going to get seasick as the car rocked out of the parking lot.

"How old is this car?" I shouted above all the racket it was making.

Kevin acted as if he were driving a fancy limousine. "My dear, this car is so old, it doesn't have a clock on the dashboard, it has a sundial."

"Yeah," Danny added. "It's so old his insurance covers fire, theft, and Indian raids!"

We got home just as Killion arrived at our house. She'd come over to show me her new glasses, which she'd just gotten, and to tell me about her date with Jacob. But Danny was still there and she wisely chose not to discuss it in front of him.

In response to her astounded look at what we were riding in, Kevin jumped out and offered her his hand. "Allow me to help you into my new cruising machine, which is leaving soon for MacKenzie's." He helped her into the back seat, next to me.

"Hold it, Kev," I ordered. "I'd better check with Mom first." I hopped out of the car and ran up to the house, only to find a note on the door saying that they'd left Wendy with Grandmother Crocker and had gone out to dinner.

I hurried back to the car. Danny had gallantly stepped out and climbed into the back seat for me, but I knew it was really an excuse to sit with Killion, who looked especially nice tonight in her new glasses and a brown skirt and sweater that matched her eyes.

MacKenzie's was unusually crowded for a Sunday night. I tried to slide gracefully into the booth we'd chosen, but my muscles were still stiff from my brief encounter with jogging.

"Killion, were you sore when you started jogging with Kevin?" I asked. "I hurt so much, I can't sit or stand."

"If that's true, you must be lying," Kevin joked.

That seemed to break the ice between Danny and Killion as we all laughed. They'd been together with Kevin and me lots of times, but now that there was an attraction between them, everything seemed awkward and uncomfortable.

I was in the middle of a story about my experiences at the clinic and meeting Mark Logan, when Kevin started going berserk all of a sudden.

"Who is that goddess?" he gasped, clutching his heart.

I followed his gaze. Bitsy McGee had just walked in with Stacy Benson and Loni Ames. "You must mean Bitsy McGee," I said dully. "I'd introduce you, but she isn't your type." I tried not to acknowledge the pang of jealousy the sight of her had given me.

"Yes, she is my type. I can tell." Kevin continued to stare at her. "I just love her mind."

"You don't even know her." I laughed. "How can you love her mind?"

"I didn't want you to accuse me of being a male chauvinist again by saying that I love what she carries her mind around in."

He grabbed my arm. "Give me a pen. Quick!"

I dug through my purse, found a pen and handed it to him. He scribbled something on a napkin. "Let me out!" He shoved me out of the booth so he could intercept Bitsy at the jukebox. I had to grab the edge of the table to keep from sprawling on the floor.

We all watched anxiously as Kevin tried to strike up a conversation with her. It was hard to tell if he was making a good impression or not.

Finally he returned and we all pounced on him, wanting to know what had happened. "Well, I cleverly asked her if she'd accidentally dropped this napkin with my phone number written on it." He held it up, then crumbled it and stuffed it into his pocket.

"Obviously she hadn't." I smirked.

He kept staring at her. "Mmmmm," he moaned. "She has the kind of lips I like. One on the top and one on the bottom."

A few couples got up to dance to music from the jukebox. "Wish me luck." Kevin grinned as he smoothed down his hair. "Here goes round two." He jumped up, then casually sauntered over to the booth where the girls were sitting and asked Bitsy to dance. She accepted.

I turned my attention back to Danny and Killion, who were both being unusually quiet. I figured it was up to me to get the conversation going again. "Do you dance?" I asked Danny.

"The last time I stepped out on a dance floor," he answered, "people started making fun of me. Next time I think I'll take a girl along with me." He turned to Killion. "Will you dance with me?"

Killion actually blushed as he took her hand and pulled her up out of the booth. I was glad. She and Danny were two of my favorite people, and I thought it would be neat if they started dating. I really didn't know Jacob very well, and it looked like I'd have to wait until tomorrow to hear about Killion's date with him.

I slouched down in the booth, feeling terribly conspicuous because I'd been left there alone while everyone else was dancing. Whenever we went to informal school dances, Killion and I had an agreement that we both had to be asked to dance at the same time or we would decline. That prevented one of us from feeling like a wallflower—the way I was feeling right now. But I knew tonight the circumstances were different.

I was extremely relieved when the pizza finally arrived and I could turn my attention to that. I wondered fleetingly what Michael Farrah would do if he knew Bitsy was out dancing with my brother.

I looked over at them, smiling at each other as they twirled around the dance floor, and noticed for the first time how much Kevin's weight lifting and jogging had paid off. He was starting to look muscular instead of scrawny. He looked good, I thought.

Bitsy looked good, too. Maybe dazzling would be a better word. She was wearing a deep lavender jumpsuit, with a cluster of violets in her hair. I wondered how she could come up with fresh violets on a Sunday night.

When the song ended, they all returned to the booth, including Bitsy. Kevin squashed me up against the wall to make room for her.

There was a moment of uncomfortable silence as everyone dived for a piece of pizza. Kevin introduced all of us to Bitsy, and she actually remembered me from English class. I was surprised she had noticed anyone beyond Michael Farrah.

"So, Bitsy," Kevin began. "I've been dying to meet you. I've heard so little about you." Everyone laughed except Bitsy. "Tell me about yourself."

She absently touched the violets with one hand. "I'm originally from New York."

"What part?" Danny asked.

"All of her," Kevin retorted.

Bitsy continued, ignoring the joke. "We moved here from Long Island a few weeks ago. I like your high school. They offer a lot of English, literature, and writing classes, and I'm into writing poetry."

"Oh, no," Danny interrupted. "She's taken a turn for the verse." We all groaned—except Bitsy again. She seemed so serious in spite of her bouncy image. I couldn't help feeling that the little speech she was giving us had been rehearsed.

Even though I was having mixed emotions about all

this, I still didn't want Bitsy to think we were laughing at her, so I tried to act serious, too. "What kind of poetry do you write?" I asked her.

"Lately I've been writing Haiku."

"What?" Kevin asked.

"Haiku," I repeated.

"Gesundheit!" Danny exclaimed.

"Sounds like a method of self-defense," Kevin added.

I gave him a piercing look. "It's a form of poetry," I said slowly, trying to use the same tone of voice Mom used when she wanted us to stop doing something.

"Can you earn a black belt in Haiku?" he asked, laughing.

I whispered into his ear, "Kev, you're overdoing it." Then I leaned around him. "Bitsy, you'll have to forgive my brother and Danny. They're a little crazy." She still didn't even crack a smile.

I couldn't believe Kevin was continuing to joke when Bitsy obviously wasn't finding it funny at all. I watched him tearing a paper cup to shreds. That's it, I thought. He's nervous around her, just like I am around Michael Farrah. Kevin's trying to make a good impression, but he's blowing it instead. Suddenly I wanted to help him. I didn't like some girl turning my brother into melted butter.

But it was too late. Stacy and Loni appeared at that instant. "We're leaving now, Bit. Are you coming with us?" Loni asked, ignoring the rest of us.

Before Kevin could react, Bitsy jumped up and took off. "I'll walk you to your car, Ms. McGee," he said politely to us, since she was already halfway to the door. He jumped up and followed her. "Round three!" he called back over his shoulder.

By the time we'd finished the rest of the pizza, he'd returned.

"You struck out, didn't you?" Danny asked, licking his fingers.

"I got a real kick out of walking her to the car. Her boyfriend was out there. He tried to kick me."

At that instant, I looked up and saw Michael Farrah and Stan Jenson walking in. Great, I thought. That's all I need—my brother and the love of my life fighting over the same girl.

"I wouldn't want to marry a girl like that," Danny said.

"Why not?" asked Kevin.

"She'd probably want to wear the plants in the family. . . ."

Chapter 14

It seemed like the only time I saw Killion anymore was when we walked to school together in the mornings. She worked at the card store on Mondays and Wednesdays after school, and now I was going to the clinic and to exercise classes on Tuesday and Thursday afternoons.

Her date with Jacob sounded very impressive. He'd taken her out to eat at a fancy restaurant where she'd ordered the diet dish du jour, and then to the theater. He'd even sent her a bouquet of forget-me-nots, timed to precede his arrival by ten minutes. Pretty smooth.

I'd gotten the distinct feeling Jacob liked to flaunt his money, or rather, his parent's money. It was an act that was not wasted on Killion. I was surprised to see this new side of her. I didn't know she could be so impressed by money. That's going to be a tough act for Danny to follow, I thought sadly.

It didn't take long for the newness of the school year to wear off and the drudgery to set in. I was so caught up in my volunteer job at the clinic, pulling together the research data for my speech, and going to exercise class with Jenny, that the week flew by. Friday night arrived before I'd had a chance to schedule in enough time to adequately worry about Austin. It suddenly hit me during the last period of the day that this was it. My date with him was approaching fast and there was no way I could get out of it a second time.

Why did I want to get out of a date with a guy like Austin? I wanted to find someone to care about and to go out with, but I just hated that feeling of insecurity—not knowing what to say or do, or even what to wear. Maybe I should have listened to Killion after all and read more of her romance novels.

I desperately wanted Austin to like me, but how could he like me if I acted too young or didn't know what to do? It bothered me when I realized I also wanted him to like me so I could keep up with Killion and have a boyfriend just because she did.

By the time school was over and we'd started walking home, I'd disintegrated into a nervous wreck. "What fun is there in dating," I wailed, "if you feel like you're going to throw up before your date arrives?"

"You'll do fine, Crock. I know you will," Killion consoled me. "I was a little nervous before Jacob arrived, but once we left, I loosened up, and we had a great time."

"But you can always come up with clever things to say, and I can't," I argued. "Plus, you see Jacob every day. I never see Austin."

"Yes, but you've gotten to know him over the phone."

"That's different. It seemed so safe to talk to him, not knowing what we both looked like. Now we have to deal with each other face to face, and . . ."

"You're afraid he won't like you in person."

"Yeah, I guess. Can I live up to the girl he thinks I am?"

"Did you pretend to be somebody you weren't on the phone?"

"No."

"Then just be the same. Actually, you're lucky. He was attracted by your 'internals,' not your 'externals.' My dad would like that."

I reached up and banged my fist against a low-hanging branch as we passed under a tree. "It was so easy to talk to him when I assumed he looked like a jerk. Now that I know he's a hunk, I just want him to think—"

"That you're a goddess?"

I groaned. Somehow I'd never considered myself goddess material.

We arrived at my house and sat down on the front porch steps to continue our conversation.

"What I'm *really* worried about, Kill, is what happens when Austin brings me home? I'll be alone with him in his car. We pull up in front of my house, and then what? He's nineteen. He's probably dated about ninety-five girls by now, and I'll have to pretend I've dated a lot of guys, too. Or at least act like I know what I'm doing.

"Should I jump out of the car the minute he stops? Should I wait until he walks around and opens the door? And what do you do when you get to the front porch? Do I start digging for my keys then? Or should I have them out already? What do I say? What if he tries to kiss me good night? What if he doesn't?"

Killion was cracking up as I became more and more agitated.

"Don't laugh at me," I pleaded. "Tell me what *you* did when Jacob took you home."

"Nothing. We left the theater and drove straight home."

"He didn't try to take you parking?"

"Crocker, we couldn't. If I'm not home by eleven, my dad rents out my room. Jacob just walked me to the door, we said, 'see ya,' and that was it."

"He didn't even try to kiss you?"

"Not at the door. I think the porch light unnerved him. But he did kiss me while we were waiting in front of the theater."

"He did? Tell me all about it!"

"There's nothing to tell. He just leaned over and kissed me. That's all."

"No fireworks?"

"No. But a police car with a siren whizzed by right at that instant. Does that count?"

"No." I laughed. "I think it's supposed to be fireworks—not sirens."

"Wait a minute." She hesitated, then dug into her backpack and pulled out one of her romance novels. "I've got a great idea. I just finished reading this novel, *Love from France*. There's a scene in it where the guy takes the girl home. I'll read it to you so you'll know how Loralee handled the same situation."

"Loralee?"

"She's the heroine. They all have names like that. Her boyfriend is a foreign exchange student from France. His name is pronounced 'Frah-swah.' The French teacher at school told me." Killion flipped through the book until she found the right spot and began to read with great dramatic feeling.

"*François turned the key in the ignition and the soft purr of the engine faded away, leaving only the sound of their breathing. He pulled Loralee toward him, a bit gruffly. His urgency, they both knew, was because his time in America was fast coming to an end, and he must soon leave his beloved Loralee and return to the green, misty hills of his homeland.*

"*They were totally enveloped in darkness, feeling as if they were the only two people in the entire world, and all that mattered was each other.*

" '*Loralee,*' *he whispered softly, his lips seeking out hers.*

"*Her pulse pounded loudly in her ears. She was afraid of the emotions welling up inside of her like a tidal wave. 'I must go in,' she gasped breathlessly.*

"*François released her reluctantly. He opened his door and pulled her out with him. Swinging her up into his manly arms, he carried her strongly and steadily to the front door. Slipping off his jacket, he carefully wrapped it around the porch light and twisted it until the annoying, glaring light died, leaving the porch bathed in sensual darkness.*

"*He pulled her to him once again, and murmured into her hair,* 'Ma chérie. Je t'aime beaucoup.'

"*It drove her crazy when he whispered love words to her in French. It was the language of love. 'I love you, too, my darling. Very much,' she sighed.*

" 'Ce soir, c'est magnifique!'

" '*Yes, tonight has been magnificent,*' *she agreed, tingling all over.*

"*His arms tightened around her. His kisses became more urgent.* 'Reviens en France avec moi,' *he pleaded desperately.*

"Loralee pushed away from him, clutching at his sweater with her dainty hand.

" 'Oui?' *he persisted, his lips almost persuading her.*

" 'No!' *Tears filled her sad eyes. 'I cannot return to France with you, my darling. It would break my mama's heart. She's gravely ill, you know. She needs me now. . . .'*

"He cupped her face in his hands. 'Je t'adore, je t'aime, je t'adore,' *he repeated over and over until she became dizzy with his nearness. She fumbled for the door, swooping quickly inside. Touching his hair one last time, she whispered softly,* 'Good-bye, my love. . . .'

" 'Au revoir, mon amour.'

"She heard his voice crack as she closed the door and crumpled to the floor in sweet tears."

Killion paused to let the emotion sink in. She blotted her eyes and gave me a mushy look. It had been hard not to snicker during her dramatic presentation.

"You really think I can use any of that?" I tried to keep a straight face.

"Can't you see the usefulness of it?" she asked, wide-eyed. "Now you know what Loralee did in a similar situation. At least you have that to build on and learn from. You can take this information and reshape it to fit your present circumstances. See why romance novels are so helpful?"

"Sure, Kill." I had to go inside before I cracked up and hurt her feelings. "Thanks for sharing that with me. I'll call you in the morning."

I swooped quickly inside, closed the door, and crumpled to the floor in sweet laughter. I sure hope I get a chance to be Loralee in my next life.

I showered and shampooed my hair as quickly as I could before dinner, but then took a good ten minutes trying to decide which type of "mood cologne" to wear. Did I want to smell woodsy or wild animaly? I decided woodsy sounded safer.

I was starving to death, but that knot had returned to my stomach, making it impossible to eat. I succeeded in rearranging the food on my plate cleverly enough to fool Mom and Dad into thinking I'd actually eaten some of it. One of the articles I'd read pointed out that it was good manners to carry breath mints with you on a date, so I'd bought five rolls of them to take with me tonight. I figured if I got *really* hungry, I could survive on breath mints until I got home.

It'd taken me days to decide what outfit to wear for my date with Austin. I finally settled on rust-colored jeans with a matching striped shirt, but it still took me a while to get dressed and "wake up" my look with accessories. Luckily, my hair turned out right on the first try. Finally I was ready. Now all I had to do was sit still for an hour and a half so I wouldn't mess up my hair or wrinkle my clothes before he arrived. I put my song on the stereo to help shorten the wait.

Suddenly the doorbell was ringing and I knew he was there. My insides felt exactly the same as they feel whenever I get called on in class to answer a question and I don't know the answer. This is hardly the same thing, I thought as I heard myself introducing Austin to my family.

I'd planned on being prepared so I could whisk him out the door before he was grilled by my mother, but I'd forgotten my jacket. Kevin followed me as I hurried back down the hallway to get it. I whispered to him, "Not bad for a wrong number, is he?"

"Aw, he's okay, I guess," Kevin said, yawning as if he were bored. "I have a mustache too, you know."

I scoffed at him. "You do? Where?"

"Right here." He pointed to his upper lip. "I just keep *mine* shaved off, that's all."

"Cute." I grabbed my jacket. Kevin had been growing a mustache for about seventeen years and he didn't even have a shadow yet.

Austin ushered me out the door and into his car. I was glad to see he had bucket seats so I didn't have to worry about how close to sit to him.

"Hello, again, Emily Crocker." He smiled over at me as he started up his car. He looked great tonight in an emerald-colored sweater that made his eyes look even greener. He smelled good, too, like musk aftershave.

He gave me the once-over. "You certainly do look different from the last time I saw you," he said, smirking.

"Better, I hope."

His answer was only a chuckle. "I'm glad you're a blond," he said.

I wondered why the color of my hair mattered at all. Did that mean he would have been disappointed if he'd met me two weeks ago—before my hair had been "sun-painted"?

He maneuvered his car smoothly onto the freeway, driving a little too fast, I thought. "Gotta change our plans for tonight."

"Oh? Did you get called in to work again?"

"No, it's not that. I finally found an apartment and started moving today. I've almost finished getting all my stuff in. Some friends are coming over to help me get settled." He reached over and took my hand. "I'd like you to help, too. We'll catch a movie some other night, okay?"

"Sure." I slouched down in the seat and wondered what my mom would say if she knew I'd be spending the evening at a guy's apartment. I felt guilty, but I really shouldn't have because I honestly hadn't known that Austin was going to change our plans.

I felt panicky, like the evening was out of my control. I wanted to be back home, where it was safe. I barely knew Austin, and now I was going to spend the evening with his friends, who were probably older, like he was. What should I do? I didn't want him to think I was a baby.

I stared out the window as we drove, worrying about the definite lag in our conversation. I couldn't think of a single thing to talk about. But small talk just didn't seem important right now. I was more worried about what I was getting myself into.

Why hadn't I just told my parents all the facts about Austin? I didn't lie to them, but I didn't tell them everything either. They probably would have strongly requested that I not date him. Sure, I would have been mad at them, and Austin would have definitely thought I was too young then. But at least I'd be at home right now instead of flying down the freeway to who knows what.

Chapter 15

Austin's apartment was in a part of town I wasn't very familiar with. We found a place to park on a dark side street and walked a block to his building. He draped his arm casually across my shoulders as we walked. I got the impression it was something he would have done no matter what girl he was with.

Conversation between us was still strained, not at all like it was on the phone. I wished frantically that we could just spend some time alone, getting to know each other, before we had to appear in public as a "couple."

Loud voices were coming through his door as he opened it. Inside, a guy and two girls were unpacking boxes of books and dishes.

" 'Bout time you got here, Brandt," the guy hollered to Austin as he raised a beer in salute. He looked even older than Austin and had a full beard. "Let's get your stereo unpacked and hooked up so we can have some good music."

"Sure, Chuck," Austin replied.

The girls called me into the kitchen. They both had blond hair and were wearing jogging outfits.

"You must be Emily," one of the girls said. "I'm Jody, and this is Rene." The name "Rene" reverberated through my brain like a gunshot as she continued, "We were jogging by when Austin grabbed us and put us to work. This kitchen is disgusting, so here you go." She tossed me a sponge and turned her attention back to Rene and their discussion of how they were fixing up their own apartment.

I stood there, holding the sponge and feeling ridiculous. I glanced at Austin in the other room. He smiled and waved, then went back to work on the stereo. Slipping off my jacket, I watched Rene trying to keep her balance as she stood on a chair to sponge off the top shelf of the cupboards. She kept giggling and looking to see if the guys were watching her, which, I noticed, they were. Her blond hair hung below her waist, and her face looked freshly scrubbed, not needing any makeup at all. She was thin, like me, but somehow it looked better on her. She was certainly pretty.

Austin's comment, "I'm glad you're a blond," came back to me. He must collect them, I thought as I noticed that my hair was almost the same shade of blond as both the other girls' hair.

I had an immediate feeling of dislike for Rene, which really wasn't fair because I didn't even know her. I guessed it was jealousy. If Austin was dating someone as pretty as she was, why did he even bother with me after he saw what I looked like?

Plus, these girls were obviously in college if they shared an apartment. Austin knew I was still in high school. It was confusing. I couldn't come up with one good reason why he'd want to date me. Reluctantly I got down on my knees and began cleaning the lower cabinets, wondering whether or not Loralee had scrubbed François' kitchen on their first date. . . .

"What year are you in?" Jody asked me suddenly. I knew she meant what year of *college*, but I just answered, "sophomore," without explaining.

Jody's hair was a little shorter than Rene's, and was pulled straight back into one long braid. I noticed she had a bad complexion and tried to cover it up with a lot of makeup, which looked terrible under the harsh kitchen light. I hoped my skin didn't look that bad. I didn't like to wear too much makeup, and really didn't have to now because my skin was beginning to improve, thanks to my faithful applications of medicine.

Suddenly the door opened and about ten more people came in, making a lot of noise. Jody and Rene rushed out of the kitchen and left me sitting there on my knees. I rose up to look over the countertop and saw everyone hugging and kissing. I wondered irritably why Austin was kissing Rene when she'd already been there.

Chuck raised his voice over the noise. "I drank the last beer an hour ago. I thought the cavalry would never get here with more supplies."

Everyone laughed while he carried the beer into the kitchen, almost tripping over me. I stood up to get out of his way. He started going berserk because he couldn't find a bottle opener. His loudness was attracting everyone's attention toward us, right when all I wanted was to blend in with the crowd. I quickly scrounged around in the boxes until I found a bottle opener, then practically threw it at him to get him to shut up.

I went back to scrubbing the cabinets, not wanting to just stand and stare at everyone. It was evident that Austin was not into formal introductions, which made me feel even more like an outsider. I also noticed that all the girls who'd just arrived were blonds, except for one with long dark hair. I gathered she was Chuck's girlfriend, since she followed him into the kitchen and put her arms around him. I smiled at her but she didn't smile back.

Chuck thrust a beer at me. "Here . . . uh . . . what was your name?"

"Emily," I said, standing up.

"Emily," he repeated.

"No thanks, I don't care for one."

"Well then, *I'll* take it." The girl with the dark hair reached over and intercepted the bottle, staring me down.

Austin appeared, saving me from this awkward moment, and grabbed a beer for himself.

"Your girlfriend won't drink with us," Chuck chided him. "What's the matter? Isn't she eighteen yet?"

"Sure she's eighteen," Austin replied, tilting the beer bottle and taking a long drink. He slipped his arm around me, acting a little too familiar. "Aren't you?"

"No." My voice was barely a whisper. He knew I couldn't be eighteen. Why did he say that? I wondered if he'd gotten me mixed up with another one of his blonds.

"Then you're *almost* eighteen," he stated.

"No."

"You're almost seventeen?" Chuck asked with a sneer on his face.

"Sure," I stammered, giving in.

"All right! Now we're gittin' somewhere," Chuck joked, a little too loudly. "When will you be seventeen?"

I didn't like being made fun of, especially by Austin's unfriendly friends. I replied weakly, "I'll be seventeen in about . . . fourteen months."

They all laughed at me. Chuck pulled his girlfriend out of the kitchen. "Robbing the cradle again, Brandt?" he called back over his shoulder.

My face burned. I didn't belong here and no one was trying to make me feel welcome.

"You okay?" Austin lifted my chin and looked at me.

I shrugged my shoulders, not looking at him. What could I say? Of course I wasn't okay. But it wasn't as if we were at a party we could just leave. First of all, it wasn't a party, and second, it was Austin's apartment.

"I think I'd like to go home." I was surprised to hear my voice shaking.

He looked disappointed. "Just stay a little longer. We're almost through and then we can all sit down and listen to some music. It'll be fun; you'll see."

"Austin!" Rene called suddenly from across the room. "I found the sheets. Come help me make the bed!"

He took me by the shoulders and said again softly, "Just a little longer." Then he pretended to run across the room in an exaggerated manner so he could follow Rene into his bedroom. Everyone seemed to think it was hilarious.

I found the bathroom and locked myself in. Sitting on the edge of the bathtub, I gave in to the tears. How come everything was working out so well for Killion and not for me? We'd both gone out on our first major date, and hers had been fantastic while mine was obviously a disaster. How had I ended up in a crowd of college kids anyway? At least I was lucky that my original first date with Austin hadn't worked out. He would have been bored to death, spending last Saturday night at my house, drinking hot cocoa.

I stopped crying and started laughing. It was so stupid. Here I sat in the bathroom while Austin was in the bedroom with Rene. I wished I could climb out the little window above the bathtub and run home.

Someone started pounding on the door. "Hurry up in there! There's a lot of serious beer drinkers out here who are waiting in line!"

Embarrassed, I quickly blotted my eyes on the towel so it didn't look as if I'd been crying. I stood up tall, took a deep breath, and walked out.

Austin had apparently finished whatever he'd been doing in the bedroom and was looking for me. "There you are," he said as he grabbed my hand and pulled me aside. "We're taking a break 'cause Chuck and some of the guys brought over their electric guitars to hook up to my amps. Go sit down, and I'll be there in a second."

I stopped by the kitchen to grab a Coke. I'd seen some in the refrigerator, and I thought I might feel more comfortable if I had something in my hand to drink like everyone else, even though they were drinking beer.

"Hey, Crocker!" Chuck called. "Come sit down!" I climbed over a few people and sat on the couch near him. He and some of the other guys had hooked up two lead guitars and a bass guitar to the amps and had started to jam.

"Crocker!" Chuck called again. "I said, come sit down!"

Startled, I followed his gaze to Rene. Of course! He'd been talking to her—not to me. I'd forgotten we both had the same last name—which was how this whole thing started in the first place. Chuck hadn't known my first name, so how could he have possibly known my last name? He wanted Rene to sit on the couch—not me. I felt really stupid.

Austin was flitting here and there, trying to be a good host and making sure everyone had something to drink. I watched Rene following him around, just like a little puppy. Finally, he stopped and came to sit with me on the couch, slipping his arm around my shoulders.

I'd gotten the impression he didn't want anyone to know he was supposed to be with me tonight. But I must have been wrong or he wouldn't have put his arm around me, ignoring Rene, who sat at his feet with a hurt puppy look on her face.

I leaned back against him and turned my attention toward the music. The jam session had been rather loud at first, but then the guys toned it down and began to pick out some familiar songs. I finally started to relax and enjoy myself for the first time all evening.

Some of the people around me began to sing, so I joined in, too. It was fun. Austin leaned over and whispered, "You not only smell fantastic, but you sing fantastic."

I felt myself blushing. I knew I sang well. That was one thing I did feel confident about.

"Do you know how to play guitar?" he asked.

I nodded absently.

"Hold it! Hold it!" he hollered. The music stopped and so did my heart. What was he doing?

"Let Emily play your guitar," he ordered one of the guys. "She's good."

"No!" I protested. "I don't know how to play an *electric* guitar. I just have a regular one—an acoustic."

"Oh, it's just the same," explained Chuck, "only louder."

Austin shoved me up off the couch, and before I knew it, his friend had swung the guitar over my head and adjusted the shoulder strap.

"What kind of music do you play?" Chuck asked as he tuned his guitar.

I panicked. "Um, mostly old Beatle songs," I stammered, hoping they didn't think I was out of it.

"Great." Chuck strummed a lead-in to one song that luckily I knew. I joined right in, thankful that I'd practiced recently.

My voice blended nicely with the guys' voices as we went from one song to another. I'd been watching Chuck closely so I could follow his lead, but suddenly I became aware that no one else was singing. I glanced around the room. Everyone had stopped to listen to us, and they were all smiling at me! Except Rene. Austin gave me a wink.

I couldn't believe I was singing and playing in front of a roomful of people I didn't even know, and that I hadn't come totally unglued. I'd even forgotten about my braces! It must have been because Austin hadn't given me time to get nervous and worry about all the possible things that could go wrong, like I usually did.

After a while, I sensed it must be getting late. The next time I caught Austin's attention, I pointed to my watch, and he nodded. Amid protests, I returned the guitar to its owner and found my jacket. Several people complimented me on my singing and said they hoped to see me again. It was flattering!

I'd felt so inadequate, insecure, and *young* at the beginning of the evening, but was now feeling quite good about myself. I'd gained a little confidence during the course of events. That is, until we got into Austin's car. He and I barely said two words to each other all the way home. Was he sorry he took me to his apartment where the rest of his friends were? Did I embarrass him? But my singing and playing had been his idea. By the time we pulled up in front of my house, all those doubts about not knowing what to do had settled back over me like a heavy blanket.

Austin pulled me toward him and kissed me hard. His mustache tickled. It was nice, but no fireworks. I listened for a police siren. No siren. All I could hear was a barking dog. I didn't even feel my "pulse pounding loudly in my ears." It struck me funny and I started to giggle.

"What's so funny?" he asked, acting insulted that I'd giggled. "Didn't you have a good time?"

"*C'est magnifique,*" I replied.

He kissed me again. I pulled back, clutching at his sweater with my dainty hands. "I must go in," I tried to gasp breathlessly.

As he got out of the car, I scooted over to follow, only to have the door slammed in my face. I tried to climb gracefully back over the gearshift lever to my side of the car before he noticed. I was disappointed that he didn't carry me to the front door in his manly arms, but at least it gave me time to dig through my purse for the key.

The front light glared annoyingly, but he didn't seem to prefer the porch bathed in sensual darkness.

"Now that you know where I live," he whispered, "come over some time."

"Oh, I couldn't," I replied dramatically. "My mama, she needs me. . . ."

He looked at me oddly.

Touching his hair, I sighed softly, *"Au revoir."*

"Why are you speaking French all of a sudden?" he asked, pulling away to stare at me.

I swooped quickly through the door, closed it, and crumpled to the floor in sweet relief.

Chapter 16

During the next few weeks life got hectic with school, the clinic, and exercise class. Austin still called, but just to talk. He hadn't asked me out again.

We seemed to have a double relationship. We could talk comfortably over the phone, but had nothing to say to each other when we were together. After a while I realized I wasn't even enjoying his calls anymore because all we talked about was him—his job, his apartment, his friends, and his problems. He never asked me anything about myself. He never even mentioned my singing in front of his friends.

I felt a little guilty because sometimes when I was playing captive audience to Austin's long monologues, I wasn't sure I even liked him as a boyfriend, or if I wanted to go out with him again. In spite of my mixed emotions, it still made life more interesting to have a boyfriend than not to have one. Especially one as good-looking as he was. Killion said it sounded like Austin belonged to the "blond-of-the-month club," and wanted to make me a new selection.

I couldn't wait for the two afternoons a week that I worked at the clinic. Winter was definitely the busy time of the year and I loved the hustle and bustle. The staff handled everything so efficiently—especially the frequent emergencies they had to deal with. The doctors seemed pleased with my work. At least all the comments I'd received from Jenny were good.

But the best part about working at the clinic was Mark Logan. I didn't even know he went to my high school. He was a senior and took a lot of independent study classes which allowed him to finish early at school and be at the clinic by noon.

Mark and I worked together but could seldom talk because we were just too busy. He was always staring at me, which made me feel uncomfortable, but secretly I liked it. He treated me so much nicer than Austin did. And I thought he was kind of cute. So did Jenny, and she constantly pointed it out to me. He wasn't gorgeous like Austin, but did that really matter? Was I being too influenced by "externals" instead of "internals"?

Mark and I didn't really become good friends until he helped me avoid a major conflict in my life. I'd been taking the bus as close as I could to the clinic, then walking the rest of the way. As the winter days got shorter, and darkness came earlier, my parents insisted that I give up my volunteer job since they'd assumed it was only temporary anyway.

I'd panicked because I loved working there and didn't want to give it up. Mark found me moping around on what would have been my last day. When I explained the situation to him, I couldn't stop the tears. Luckily we were in the back so none of the patients could see.

My tears seemed to embarrass him more than they did me. He opened a box of tissues from the supply cabinet, made me sit down, and began patting my head to console me.

As I finished telling him the problem, a look of alarm spread across his face. He dropped down on one knee so we could see eye to eye.

"You mean you'd never come to the clinic anymore?"

Sniffing, I shook my head no.

"I wouldn't get to see you again?"

I kept on shaking my head. I hadn't thought of that. I knew I'd miss seeing him, too.

He pulled off his glasses. "What time do you get out of school?"

"Two-thirty."

"How about letting me pick you up at school and bring you to the clinic?"

I stared at him. He twirled his glasses around absently as he watched me, then quickly shoved them back on.

"Are you serious?"

"Sure." He grinned. "I get a break during the afternoon and I can't think of a better way to spend it than with you . . . uh, I mean, than coming to get you."

"You wouldn't mind?"

"No. I want to. Just pretend we're carpooling."

"Then I'd owe you money for gas."

"Naw."

"Yes. I insist."

"How about if you just saved it up and took me out to dinner some time?" He abruptly stood up and began to straighten the supply cabinet.

"You mean it?" I wondered briefly about his sudden attack of neatness.

He glanced back at me and nodded. "Is it a deal?"

"Yes! I mean, if it's okay with my parents, it's a deal." I jumped up and leaned over to kiss him on the cheek in my excitement, but only got as high as his chin. Feeling quite stupid by what I'd done, I whipped around and headed for the door to the reception area. Glancing back over my shoulder, I saw Mark standing there motionless, a wide grin on his face.

The big news around school now was the introduction of the first all-school talent show. It was dreamed up by student council for the purpose of creatively channeling the excess energy inspired by the holiday season—energy that was usually spent on pranks around the school. The show was to be the climax of the Christmas season, taking place on the last day before break.

I was first to arrive at lunch and was carefully unwrapping my sandwich when Killion and Jacob joined me. Once Jacob had staked his claim for Killion, the other guys, including Danny, had backed off, so I was now able to eat my lunch again.

Jacob and I ignored each other. Maybe he sensed my irritation at his constant reminders of how rich he was. It impressed Killion, but not me. I thought it was just an act.

Killion, still dieting, pulled the lid off a container of salad and licked her fingers. "Are you going to audition for the talent show?" she asked me.

"Who? Me?" I hadn't even thought of the possibility.

"Yes, you! Crocker, you have such a great voice. You could sing and play the guitar, and—"

"No, thank you," I interrupted. "I don't perform in public."

"But what about at Austin's apartment?"

"Shhhh!" I looked around quickly to see if Kevin was near. I hadn't told anyone but Killion about going to Austin's apartment and singing in front of his friends. "Subject closed," I stated.

To my relief, Jacob finished eating and left, leaving Killion and me alone for the first time in quite a while.

"Ginger," I began slowly, "Kevin tells me that Jacob and Danny are no longer on speaking terms with each other."

She took a big bite of salad so she wouldn't have to answer.

I leaned closer. "They *used* to be good friends, and now they're enemies—because of *you!*"

She didn't answer again. Out of the corner of my eye, I could see Danny watching her as he did every day. "I thought you liked Danny," I persisted.

"I do," she snapped.

"Well then?"

"Well then, what? I'm going out with Jacob now. Jacob is so . . . so . . ."

"Wealthy," I said flatly.

"So, what's wrong with that? Jacob is different. More mature."

"Egotistical," I added, motioning for Danny to come over the next time Killion looked the other way.

Danny accepted the invitation, scooping up his lunch and hurrying over. He sat down next to Killion, surprising her. She seemed unduly flustered.

The conversation lagged. I tried to think of a way to get it going the fun way it usually went when the two of them got together.

"Danny, did you hear the joke about the rope?"

Killion glared at me. I decided it'd be a good time to disappear. Picking up my things to leave, I winked at Danny. "Oh, skip it."

Mark picked me up after school, as planned, and we headed for the clinic. Conversation never lagged when I was with him.

I told him about the research I'd been doing on the topic of health and about the speech I had to give the next day. He listened attentively, leaning close to me as if he didn't want to miss one single word, and giving his advice and support. He was so sweet.

"Do you have a boyfriend?" he blurted out suddenly, his blue eyes clouding over.

He'd caught me by surprise, and I didn't know what to say. "I . . . uh . . . sort of," I answered weakly, thinking about Austin. "I'm glad we're friends though," I said to him softly.

He looked the other way. "Me, too."

It was one of the craziest days yet at the clinic. The roads were wet, causing a rash of accidents that sent us a steady stream of patients complaining of various bumps and scrapes. More serious injuries were taken to the emergency room at the hospital.

I felt like I was running in high gear, rushing back and forth through the swinging door as I signed in patients out front and helped Mark in the back. We unwrapped, delivered, and disposed of supplies as the doctors barked their commands.

Suddenly, in the middle of it all, someone grabbed my arm and pulled me aside. Looking up, I was completely startled to see Austin, of all people.

"Austin!" I exclaimed, staring at him. I hadn't seen him since our date several weeks ago. "What are you doing here? How'd you even know I worked here?" I added, realizing just how little he knew about me because he never asked.

He kept hold of my arm, squeezing it a little too tightly. "My dad told me you worked here," he explained. "He's a doctor."

"I know." I'd run into Dr. Brandt once when I'd taken some paperwork over to the main hospital. I'd known who he was instantly because of the strong family resemblance.

"Emily, tell them you're leaving and come with me." He motioned toward Jenny.

"I can't leave now."

"Why not? You're just a volunteer."

"Austin, we're incredibly busy right now. Look around you. They need me."

He mimicked me. "They *need* you? Well, so do I."

I held my ground and he relented.

"Oh, all right." He sighed irritably. "What about tonight? I'll pick you up."

"Emily!" Mark's voice made me jump. I whipped around. He was standing in the doorway. "There's been a bus accident. We're handling the overflow of patients from the emergency room. We need to hand carry several pints of blood from the main hospital or the clinic's supplies will run low. Come on!" He glared at Austin.

I turned back around. "Austin, I can't go out tonight. I've got a speech to give tomorrow in English and I have to prepare. . . ."

"You've got to," he demanded, acting annoyed at my hesitation. "I need you tonight."

"I need you right now!" Mark's voice was urgent.

Suddenly I felt furious at Austin. He was so selfish! He didn't care that I had something important to do. He just expected me to drop everything and rearrange my life for him. What right did he have showing up at the clinic and demanding that I leave with him?

All of a sudden I became frantic at the thought of the doctors running out of supplies because I was wasting time talking with Austin. He probably wouldn't care about that either.

"I *can't*," I insisted, wrenching my arm away from his grasp. "I have to go, Austin. *Now!*" I twirled around and ducked under Mark's arm as he held the door open for me. I didn't even look back.

*   *   *

That evening found me desperately trying to focus my attention on the presentation of my speech. The more prepared you are, Ms. Milliren had said, the less you'll have to depend on your note cards. I shut the door to my room, positioned myself in front of the mirror, and began to practice: "How is your health like a garden? The two should be cared for, nurtured, and watched over every day." Good opener, I thought. Ms. Milliren said that starting out with a question would grab everyone's attention.

But each time I got to the third note card, my mind would be back on Austin again. He'd looked so handsome standing there, telling me that he needed me. For an instant I thought I'd say yes to anything. I even imagined a rivalry between Mark and Austin for my attention.

"That's pushing it a little, Crocker," I said to myself in the mirror. I wondered if he wouldn't like me anymore now that I'd turned him down.

Kevin stuck his head in the door. "Want to go down to MacKenzie's for a little while?"

"I can't, Kev. I've got to rehearse my speech. I haven't even written the ending yet. It's going to be terrible. And I don't know if I can come up with one thousand words either. Can I count a contraction as two words?"

Kevin shook his head. "Em, I'm sure your speech is going to be good. I'll bet you've spent more time doing research on it than anyone else in the class."

"Yeah, but I'm still worried. My last research paper was such a disaster."

He rolled his eyes.

"I'm serious. I had to rewrite it three times before it was good enough to throw away."

"You'll do fine, Em. Where's that Crocker confidence?" He saluted me. "I'll bring you back a slice of deluxe pizza—hold the anchovies."

The door closed. He was a good brother, I thought. And what problem was so gigantic that it couldn't be dealt with over a delicious slice of MacKenzie's deluxe pizza?

I sighed and faced the mirror again with renewed confidence. "Now class," I said importantly, "how is your health like a garden?"

Chapter 17

The next day at school I was a walking zombie. All I wanted was to get my speech over with. My stomach was in such a state of anxiety, I felt sick enough to go home. But then I'd just have to go through another nerve attack again the next day.

Stopping by my locker to pick up the speech, I found a note wedged in the door. It said:

Dear Emily, I caught a glimpse of you this morning in the hallway. You look beautiful today. Good luck on your speech. Knock 'em dead. Mark

I felt warm inside after reading it. He thinks I'm beautiful? I quickly folded it, put it safely inside my pocket for luck, and headed down the hall for my dreaded English class.

Secretly, I'd hoped Michael Farrah would be absent today, but unfortunately he wasn't. Sitting down at my desk, I began repeating to myself, "How is your health like a garden?" so I would at least know the first line of my speech without having to look at my note cards.

"Are you ready for this?" said a voice, breaking my concentration.

It was Bitsy. She'd been quite friendly to me ever since that night at MacKenzie's, and I liked her even though I'd convinced myself at first that I wouldn't.

"Me? Ready?" I answered, laughing. "Was Joan of Arc ready to be burned at the stake?"

"I know what you mean," she replied. "I'm so nervous I could throw up."

"You are?" I was surprised. I always assumed if I looked like Bitsy, everything in life would be easy. I somehow felt comforted by the fact she and I were sharing the same feelings.

"You'll do fine, Bitsy." We exchanged smiles as the bell rang. She returned to her desk in front of Michael Farrah, who had been watching us the whole time we talked.

Ms. Milliren's voice sounded far away as she started class. She explained that speakers would be chosen in alphabetical order. I decided it was too late to change my name to Zrocker, so I leaned back in my chair and accepted my fate. I was number four.

As the speeches began, I started having serious second thoughts about my idea of showing the class some sample exercises as part of my talk. I'd learned them at Jenny's exercise class. It'd seemed like a terrific idea about midnight last night, but now it seemed rather silly.

I'd almost reasoned myself out of it because I didn't want to be laughed at, but after yawning my way through the first three speeches I decided to go for it. At least it would wake up the class and get their attention back.

"Next—Crocker, Emily." I got so dizzy when Ms. Milliren called my name, I thought I was going to pass out. I don't even remember walking to the front of the room. My mouth felt like the Sahara Desert.

Then an amazing thing happened. As I began to tell the class about the clinic and all the exciting things that happened there, I suddenly became aware of their reactions to what I was saying. They began to sit up straighter, lean forward, and laugh at the experiences that were funny.

I got so into my talk, I kept losing my place in the note cards. I felt as if I didn't even need them anymore.

Then, as I got to the part about the sample exercises, a crazy idea flashed through my brain like electricity. "Everybody get up," I ordered. "Stand next to your desk." I didn't recognize my own voice and it startled me to see everyone jumping up to obey my command.

I described each exercise, explained what purpose it

· served, then led the class through the routine several times. Even Ms. Milliren joined in. It was great!

At the end, everyone sat down huffing and puffing while I finished my speech. Not only was I surprised by a round of applause, but the question and answer session stretched on so long Ms. Milliren had to cut it short.

"Thank you, Emily." She beamed. "That was an excellent speech."

I *do* remember walking *back* to my desk. Everyone was smiling at me. As I passed Michael Farrah's desk, he whispered, "That was great, Emily!"

The remaining speeches seemed to blur into one as I leaned back in my desk and mentally relived my moment of success.

After school, I stopped by the mall on my way home. I wanted to find a telephone and call Austin, but I wasn't sure if I had enough nerve to do it. I finally found a phone, then stared at it for about twenty minutes before I could even pick it up. I'd never called a guy before, but I had a funny feeling that I'd never hear from Austin again if I didn't call him. My fingers kept slipping off the buttons as I tried to punch in his number.

"Hi."

"Emily?" He seemed surprised, then angry. "Did you call to apologize?"

"Apologize? No, Austin. I don't have anything to apologize for. I was *working* yesterday. I didn't have time for you to hassle me."

"Hassle you? I didn't know asking you out on a date was hassling you."

"Oh, Austin, it isn't." I lowered my voice so the people strolling through the mall couldn't hear me. "It's just the way you did it. You didn't ask—you demanded. And you wouldn't listen to what I was trying to tell you about myself. You never listen when I try to talk about myself." Whoa. Slow down, I thought. I hadn't meant to say all that. It just slipped out.

He hesitated. "Where are you right now?"

"At the mall."

"Stay there. I'm coming to get you."

"Now?"

"Yeah. I'll meet you by the fountains."

"But, Austin, my mom will be wond—" Whoops, I thought. Cool the little girl bit, Crocker.

"I'll drive you home from there," he continued. "I'll be honest with you, Emily. I have a date for later tonight. But I want to see you first."

I hung up and walked through the mall. Great, I thought. Not only do I accidentally meet my boyfriend as he's *calling* another girl, but now he's going to take me home on his way to *date* another girl. I don't think this is the way it's supposed to happen. Wonder if Killion has run across that situation in any of her romance novels. I get the feeling I'm not the only girl on Austin's mind. Hope the other girl's not Rene. . . .

Sitting down on a bench by the fountains, I tried to imagine why Austin had needed me so badly last night. Not badly enough for him to cancel his date tonight with Miss Blond Somebody, I thought.

"Miss Emily? Is that you?" The familiar accent gave him away. I scooted over to make room for Mr. Lebowitz on the bench.

"Hi, Mr. Lebowitz. Are you taking a break?"

"Yes, ma'am. I left my son-in-law in charge for a few minutes—heaven help me!" he cried, throwing his hands into the air. "I can't be gone long or I may find myself bankrupt when I return."

I couldn't keep from laughing. He asked me what I was doing, sitting alone in the mall, and I explained it to him.

"You want me to wait with you until your young man comes?"

"No." I smiled up at him. "But thanks for offering. You'd better get back before your son-in-law puts your store up for sale."

He smiled, gave me a fatherly pat on the shoulder, and ambled off through the mall.

Austin arrived shortly after Mr. Lebowitz left. We sat and stared at each other for about five minutes, each starting to say something, then stopping. Here we go again, I thought. It seems we can communicate only over the phone, but not in person.

Suddenly I got an idea. I knew it was crazy, but we needed something to break the ice. I grabbed his hand. "Come on!"

He frowned but followed me down the mall to a short hallway off the main shopping area where I'd found the telephones. Two of them were mounted side by side on the wall. I picked up one of them, handed it to him, and grabbed the other one for myself.

He was staring at me like he couldn't believe what I was doing, so I turned my back to him and leaned against the wall.

"Hello? Is Austin there?"

No answer. I tried again, not looking at him. "Is this Austin?"

No answer.

"Could you please speak a little louder? I can't hear you."

He laughed and decided to play the game. Turning around, he leaned his back against mine. "This is Austin speaking. Is this crazy Emily?"

"Yes, and crazy Emily wants to know what you wanted to see her about last night that was so incredibly important."

"Emily, can I be serious for a minute?"

"Be my guest."

He paused for a moment, then went on, "Emily, when I first met you—I mean, met you over the phone, I couldn't believe how sweet and understanding you were. I felt as if I already knew you, and that I could trust you. I guess that's why I kept calling and started confiding in you. I mean, I know I talk about myself a lot, but you don't really give me advice. You just listen. You're so different from . . ." His voice trailed off.

"Rene?" I ventured, filling in the name for him.

He paused. "Yeah, Rene. And other GTG's." I felt him shift his body away from me.

"GTG's?" I didn't understand.

"I guess you wouldn't know about a thing like that; you're too sheltered. It means 'Good Time Girls.' They're just for fun. You can't talk to them. They're never serious. All the girls I've met so far at the university are like that. They're nothing like you." He hesitated. "Emily, I know you're only fifteen. . . ."

"Almost sixteen," I corrected.

"Okay, almost sixteen." He laughed. "But you're so down-to-earth. You're a real person. You're so real, it scares me."

We turned around at the same instant, facing each other, the phones still in place at our ears.

"I scare you?"

He nodded. "I've been reluctant to see you again, because I like you. I mean, I *really* like you. But you're so . . . young."

"Young?" I repeated, giving him a look which hopefully told him I wasn't believing what he was telling me. I was afraid at the beginning that he'd think I was too young, but now it didn't seem to be such a big deal anymore. Especially since I was starting to feel older than him, or at least more mature.

"Emily, I'm almost twenty. I'd like you to be my girlfriend. I need someone like you in my life. But you're probably just starting to date, and I'm not ready to . . . Well, to stop dating."

"Stop dating?" He must have thought I wanted to go steady with him! I wasn't even sure I ever wanted to talk to him again after all this he was handing me.

"Well." He leaned as close as he could without touching me. "I'm having a good time. I won't lie to you. It's just that I don't want to lose track of you. I want to keep in touch, and see you once in a while. Then, maybe when you're a little older, we can get together again."

The whole time Austin had been talking so sincerely to me, he'd been looking over my head at something in the mall. The fact that he wasn't giving me his undivided attention was beginning to annoy me, so I turned to see what he was looking at. Two girls had stopped to sit on a bench. Both were blonds.

My annoyance turned to anger. Austin couldn't even

stop looking at other girls for five minutes while he was with me. I felt disgusted with him.

He turned me back around, bent down and kissed me. I was astounded at everything he'd said. I never dreamed he liked me that much. He certainly had a funny way of showing it. Was he just playing games with me? For his own ego? I didn't know whether to laugh at him or kiss him back. The phone slipped out of my hand and clanked against the wall. He seemed sincere, but something inside of me just wouldn't let me trust him. Maybe because I knew how easily he could ignore my feelings.

"Austin," I began, not exactly sure what to say. "Are you telling me you care about me, yet you're leaving in a few minutes to go out with some other girl? One of your *blond* GTG's?" I emphasized the word "blond" to let him know I was on to him.

He shrugged his shoulders. "Okay, so I'm a creep. What can I say?" He hung up both phones and slipped his arms around my waist. "Can we stay friends?"

I always thought I'd feel all warm, happy, and breathless on the day that a guy held me in his arms and professed his feelings for me. But instead I felt nothing. I didn't want someone to care about me in a few years. I wanted someone right now. Sticking my chin out, I looked him straight in the eye. "Are you seeing Rene tonight?"

"Yeah," he whispered. "But, Emily, I hope you always stay the way you are. Don't ever turn into a Rene. Please?" He pulled me close. "Give me time. Wait until I come around to my senses. Okay?"

"I can't promise."

"Can't promise what?"

"That *I'll* be around when *you* come around."

He pulled back and looked into my eyes. He had a smug look on his face which disgusted me even further. His mustache twitched at the corners. "I think you will," he answered.

I bit my tongue to keep from saying what I really thought.

"Now come on, crazy Emily. I've got to take you home."

All the way home, I couldn't look at Austin. I didn't even try to keep the conversation from lagging this time. I felt cheated, manipulated. I had an overwhelming desire to find Mark and to cry on his shoulder. He'd listen to me. He'd understand.

I leaned back, watching the scenery fly past the window— too fast as usual. No, I thought. I couldn't tell Mark about what had just happened between Austin and me. I closed my eyes and imagined the hurt look that would come over his face. I couldn't be a jerk, like Austin, and hurt Mark's feelings.

I searched my memory for a passage out of one of Killion's romance novels that would help me this time. But, for some reason, I just couldn't picture François pulling Loralee close and professing his undying love for her, then dumping her off at home so he could go out with a French version of a GTG.

Chapter 18

Why did it seem like every weekend I found myself moping around the house, depressed about my love life? Of course, before I had one, I still spent the weekends moping around the house because I didn't have a love life.

Actually, I wasn't even thinking about Austin. I'd pretty much written him off as being undependable, selfish, and insincere. I'd been so caught up by his gorgeous looks, I'd allowed him to treat me poorly just so I could have him for a boyfriend. I vowed to myself I'd never be that desperate again. I didn't even feel hurt by him. All I felt was anger. I wasn't going to be good ole Emily, waiting for him while he was out with his Good Time Girls.

Surprisingly, I also felt a sense of success. The relationship hadn't failed because of me or my insecurities like I'd anticipated it would. He blew it. I felt like I'd lost the battle, but won the war.

I found myself thinking about Mark instead. I'd been so used to spilling out all my problems to him because he was good at listening and understanding, that I'd kind of taken him for granted. I hadn't even thanked him for the note he'd left in my locker or told him how it had calmed me down right when I needed it the most.

Funny, I thought. I'm doing to Mark just what Austin has been doing to me. How could I be so callous? I felt angry with myself and wished Mark would call me. But why should I expect that? He'd never called me before or even asked for my number. And now that he'd seen me with Austin, I was sure he'd back off.

I wandered into the kitchen where Mom was writing

Christmas cards, when a sudden loud commotion announced
Kevin and Killion's return from jogging. Looking exhausted,
they flopped down at the table to recover.

"Want something to drink?" I offered.

"Gimme a beer," Kevin huffed.

I threw him a root beer and stuck my head back into the
refrigerator. "Killion, we're all out of diet pop. Sorry."

"That's okay. I'll take a three and a half up."

"A three and a half up?"

"That means I'll split a 7-Up with you."

After they caught their breath, they both started in on
me.

"*We've* decided," Killion began, "that you would be a
big hit in the talent show and we're not going to let you
say no."

"That's right." Kevin joined in. "I've heard you practicing the guitar in your room, Em, and sometimes I can't
tell if it's you or the record. You've got that song down
perfectly."

I didn't say anything.

"Em," he continued. "I really think you should sing
'At Seventeen' in the talent show. If you're scared, I'll
back you up on guitar and so will Danny. That way, you
won't be up there on stage all alone."

He almost had me convinced. Being in front of people
didn't seem as frightening to me now as it had before
I'd given my speech and before I'd sung at Austin's
apartment. But should I sing "At Seventeen"? I couldn't
imagine standing up on stage, singing words like, "To
ugly duckling girls like me . . ." Why would I want to
declare to the entire student body that I thought I was
ugly?

I chuckled and shook my head. "I just can't, you guys.
What if no one applauds?"

"Hey," Kevin argued. "They'll not only applaud, but I
can guarantee you a standing ovation." He took a quick
swig of root beer.

"How?" I said, scoffing.

"Just sing the National Anthem."

Mom had been listening quietly all this time, but even she took sides with Kevin and Killion.

"Emily, I think you should do it. It'd be fun for you. And you've got such a lovely voice, you really should flaunt it. I know I would." She paused to lick a stamp. "Heaven knows you didn't inherit your beautiful voice from me."

I shook my head, still unsure. "I just can't help remembering that terrible talent show we had back in junior high school, and how awful most of the acts were."

"Yeah." Killion laughed. "Remember Loni Ames' little brother? He'd practiced playing the kazoo for a solid month. Then, the night of the show, he accidentally swallowed it!"

"Good thing he didn't play the piano," Kevin added.

"But, Crocker," Killion interrupted. "You're good. Who knows? You may even . . ." She paused as a thought struck her. "Wait a minute!" she cried, jumping up. "I just got a super idea. Why don't you let *Jacob* accompany you? He's got incredibly expensive equipment—electric guitars, amps, and even a set of electronic drums. He—"

"No!" I cut her off sharply. Everyone looked at me strangely, but there was no way I was going to let Jacob's money influence me the way it had Killion. "You guys almost have me convinced. Still, I'm just not sure." I paused to think it over, then added, "But if I do decide to audition, it will be with Kevin and Danny."

Killion looked hurt. Jacob had been a sore spot between us for weeks. I couldn't believe the way she'd been making a fool of herself over him at school. It was embarrassing. I'd been resisting the urge to tell her I'd seen Jacob twice with the same girl in his car—some senior. I wished Killion had been with me at the time instead of at work so she could have seen it with her own eyes.

Still, I felt sorry I'd been so rude to her. "Let's go up to my room for a while, Kill. Okay?"

She finished her pop and followed me upstairs, flopping down on the bed. We each had gotten so busy with our own lives, it seemed like it'd been ages since we'd had a good, long talk like we used to.

"Oh here, I almost forgot." Killion sat up and pulled an envelope out from under her sweatshirt with a great flourish. "It's an invitation to Jacob's party. Engraved, no less. Who are you going to invite? Austin?"

I read the invitation, which was formally addressed to Miss Crocker and Guest.

"I don't know who I'll ask." I sighed. "Maybe I'll go by myself. Or maybe I won't go at all."

"Oh, Tarrah, you've got to go. How could you pass up a chance to see Jacob's house? I've heard it's fantastic."

I looked her straight in the eye. "Is Danny invited?"

She shifted uncomfortably. "Well, of course he's invited."

"Do you really think he's going to go? If you're there with Jacob?"

"I don't know," she answered weakly.

"You do too know." I raised my voice. "Killion, if I ask you a yes-or-no question, will you answer honestly?"

"Yes."

"That wasn't the question." I stood up so I could move around for emphasis. "Now, picture yourself stranded on a desert island with Danny and Jacob." I paced back and forth like a lawyer stating my case. "All things are equal. There is no money, and the water and food have been exactly divided—"

"Is there a diet pop machine?" She cut in.

"Shut up, Killion, this is serious." I stopped to regather my thoughts. "You each live in a separate cave—all the same size and shape—no more, no less. Now the question: The guy you would spend all your time with, and who you would probably fall madly in love with, would be—*Danny!* Yes or no?

"You said you'd answer honestly," I reminded her. "Think what Loralee would say if it was her." I quickly put my hand over Killion's mouth. "And don't you dare say François."

She removed my hand and sighed. "Oh, Tarrah, she'd say yes, and I say yes, and you knew I'd say yes." She glared at me. "But I'm warning you. This isn't to go beyond this room!"

I reveled in my success. "Killion, you've got to ask Danny to take you to Jacob's party."

She continued to glare. Maybe I had gone a little overboard, but I secretly enjoyed making her confess.

"Look, Crocker." She jumped up. "Will you get off my back about Danny and Jacob? What business is it of yours, anyway? I'm going out with Jacob and that's final. With Jacob I've got a chance to change my life. What's wrong with that?" Her voice broke as she blinked away some tears. "You just don't understand how hard it is living at home right now." She quickly wiped her cheek with the back of her hand, regained her composure, then turned on me. "Look, I don't appreciate you giving me the third degree and making me say things I don't mean. Mind your own business!"

Killion yanked the door open and disappeared down the hallway. A few seconds later, I heard the front door slam.

Kevin appeared. "What happened?"

"I made her mad."

"No kidding!"

Suddenly I had a tremendous urge to see Mark. "Kev, will you drive me to the clinic? Just for a few minutes?"

I ran a comb through my hair and put on some lip gloss while we were driving. My heart felt like it weighed about ninety-five pounds. I didn't want Killion to be mad at me, but I didn't want her getting hurt over Jacob either. I felt it was my duty as her friend to get her together with Danny before Jacob messed up her life.

As Kevin pulled up in front of the clinic, my song came on the radio. Normally I would've waited for it to end before getting out, but now I didn't want to feel those depressing feelings it gave me when I listened to it.

I quickly hopped out of the car. "Wait for me. I'll just be a minute." Slipping through the door of the clinic, I found Mark working in the back. All of a sudden I didn't know what to say to him. He seemed really surprised to see me.

"What are you doing here when you don't have to be?" he asked.

"I came to see you."

"You did?"

We both stood there grinning stupidly at each other.

"Is something wrong?" he asked, his face changing to a worried look.

I started to say yes and no at the same time, and it came out "yo." "Actually, I just wanted to see if you accidentally dropped this piece of paper with my phone number written on it—" I shoved the note I'd scribbled hastily in the car on a gum wrapper at him. Sometimes it helps to have a crazy brother, I thought.

Mark looked astonished. "You want me to call you?"

"Well, as long as you've got my number, you might as well."

Suddenly Jenny flew around the corner. "Emily, hi!" She looked at Mark, then back at me. "Excuse me. I'll leave you two alone." She backed through the doorway, giving us a wink and a wave.

"I'd better get back to work," Mark said, clearing his throat. "But I'll call you as soon as I get home tonight."

My song was just ending as I slipped back into the car.

Kevin and I stopped at MacKenzie's on the way home. While he was up at the counter getting our drinks, Bitsy appeared.

"Hi, Emily!" She slid into the booth next to me. I wondered if she had noticed I was with Kevin.

"Hi," I answered. "You look great." She wore a soft yellow sweater with white jeans. One side of her hair was pulled back to reveal three yellow sweetheart rosebuds. I just couldn't resist asking her, "Where do you find fresh flowers to wear every day?"

"My uncle owns a store in the mall which sells plants and flowers. He keeps me well stocked."

"Oh." The connection clicked in my mind. "Is it Mr. Lebowitz?"

"Why, yes. Do you know him?"

I nodded and she seemed pleased. Small world, I thought as Kevin joined us. She didn't act surprised to see him. He wisely chose to keep his mouth shut this time as Bitsy and I continued our conversation about the mall, school, and English class. I was dying to bring up the topic of Michael

Farrah but was afraid to. Maybe I'd rather not know the details.

Suddenly she stopped and leaned forward. "Emily, the real reason I came over to talk to you was because somebody told me you're a good singer and you play guitar. Could we get together and work out some songs for the talent show? I sing, too, but I'm not brave enough to do it all alone up on that stage."

I hesitated, startled by the invitation, so Kevin jumped in, "Actually, Emily was already planning on auditioning. Weren't you, Em?"

Before I could answer, he went on, "My friend and I are going to accompany her on the guitar. Why don't we *all* get together and practice? That'd be four of us."

"That's okay with me!" Bitsy exclaimed.

They both looked at me. Real smooth, Kevin, I thought. Then I remembered Killion and her offer of letting Jacob take over with all of his expensive equipment. I'd show her that *I* didn't need him or his influence either.

"Well?" Kevin urged, looking as if he'd murder me if I said no.

"Sounds great," I stammered, still not believing my ears. Bouncy Bitsy McGee and Emily Crocker, together on stage. It would be incredible.

We made plans to practice the next afternoon. Kevin and I finished our drinks and started home. I had such mixed emotions. I felt sad about Killion, but I also felt excited about the talent show and especially about the fact that right now I was on my way home to wait for the phone to ring as usual. Only this time I *knew* it was going to ring. And I knew it was going to be Mark.

Chapter 19

Sitting in a booth at MacKenzie's with Mark gave me a warm glow inside. It was Saturday night and I was out on a date—even though I'd practically done the asking. I didn't feel nervous at all. Didn't even feel like throwing up before he'd arrived. Mark had been a big hit with my parents. They seemed real impressed that he worked at the clinic and took independent study courses at school.

We talked a lot about our braces and the suffering we were both enduring because of them. I made a point to listen to him for a change, but he did drag a few things out of me, like the fact that I'd had a fight with Killion. I also told him a little about Austin, but I left out the part about how we'd met. It wasn't exactly something I wanted everyone to know.

Scanning the restaurant, I noticed everyone seemed to be there. Kevin and Danny were in a booth near us. Bitsy, Loni, and Stacy (or the three goddesses, as Danny had dubbed them) were in a booth by the door. Michael Farrah was sitting with some guys I didn't know. I wondered if he and Bitsy'd had a fight.

The door opened and Killion walked in with Jacob. She was hanging all over him. It was disgusting. Then she walked right past me and didn't even speak! I couldn't believe it! She ignored Kevin and Danny, too, as she led Jacob to an empty booth.

"Did you see that?" I choked, swallowing a lump in my throat. Mark reached over and grabbed my hand.

"Mark, Killion and I have been friends forever! Now she's not even going to talk to me?"

"Do you want to leave?" he asked in a sympathetic voice. It was nice being with someone who was so concerned about my feelings for a change.

"No." I sat up straight and glared in Killion's direction even though she wasn't looking. "Mark, see the way she acts with him? And he's two-timing her behind her back. How can she be so blind?"

He squeezed my hand. "She'll come around; she's got loyal friends."

"I wasn't mad at her before, even though I knew she was mad at me. But now I *am* mad. I have just as much right to be here as she does. Plus, I think she's let Jacob turn her against me. He knows I've got him figured out." Loud laughter burst from their corner of the room, probably over another one of Killion's jokes. "Well, I was going to apologize to her, but forget it."

I caught Kevin's eye and he raised his shoulders as if to say, What's going on? Danny just looked sad.

"It'll blow over," Mark consoled me. "*I* sure wouldn't want to throw away your friendship."

I gazed into his eyes. He had a way of looking inside of me, like he could tell what I was thinking or feeling. It was unnerving. And he always said the right thing at the right time. I finally had to lower my eyes. His were so intense!

A sudden loud voice interrupted us. "Emily! I've been looking all over for you!"

I jumped, jerking my head up, and was shocked to see Austin standing there.

He ignored Mark, who squeezed my hand even tighter. "I went by your house and you weren't there."

"Austin!" I exclaimed. Why was he always sneaking up and surprising me? "Um, I wasn't home because I'm here. With Mark." I glanced at Mark, who was studying Austin with narrowed eyes.

I knew Austin must have come to MacKenzie's just to find me. It was strictly a high school hangout. The college kids had their own places.

"Dance with me." Austin took hold of my free hand

and started to pull me up out of the booth. Mark held on tight to the other hand.

"Austin!" I yanked my hand back. "I'm here with *Mark!*" I repeated. "Will you just stop walking into my life and demanding that I do whatever pleases you at the moment?" There. I'd said it.

He was mad. He scowled at Mark, then turned on me. "Look, Emily," he hissed. "Just forget everything I said to you the other day. I must have been crazy to think . . ."

Mark grabbed Austin's arm and shoved him away from the table. "Leave her alone!" he shouted. "Get lost!"

The song on the jukebox ended at the same instant Mark yelled, which made it sound even louder. I froze while Austin and Mark glared at each other, their fists clenched tightly. For a second I actually thought they were going to start fighting. Finally Austin whipped around and slammed out the front door.

I felt everyone's eyes on us as I buried my head in my hands. Mark slid around to my side of the booth and put his arms around me. I couldn't believe Austin would lash out at me like that. In public, no less.

Kevin tried to help divert some of the attention away from me by starting up the jukebox again. He and Bitsy began to dance, and so did Killion and Jacob. Danny still sat there, looking forlorn. I leaned against Mark until I felt my heart beating normally again.

"What did that jerk say to you the other day?" he asked. I felt him tense up in anticipation of my answer.

"It's not important, Mark. He obviously didn't mean it, and it didn't mean anything to me either." I took a couple of deep breaths. "I think I'd like to go home now."

We drove home in silence. But it wasn't a strained silence like it was with Austin and me. It was an understanding silence.

I always wondered what it would be like to have two men fighting over me. Sounds romantic, I thought, but humiliating seemed to be a better word.

Mark stopped in front of my house, pulled me to him, and gave me a long bear hug. "Emily," he whispered into my hair. "I really like you, but if you'd rather be with that other guy, I'll back off and try to understand."

"Oh, Mark." My voice was muffled by his jacket. "I'd rather be with you."

He pulled back to look at me. "Really?"

"Really."

"You're not just saying that because I defended your honor tonight?"

"No. I mean it. But it was awfully sweet of you to do that."

"I should have done more. I should have ripped his mustache off."

I started giggling at the thought of that.

"May I kiss you?" he asked me softly.

"I've never kissed anyone who wore braces before," I whispered, suddenly feeling timid.

"Me neither."

"What if it's painful?"

"There's only one way to find out."

His kiss was soft and gentle, not painful at all. This time I didn't wonder what Loralee would have done. I did what Emily Crocker wanted to do. I kissed him back.

Chapter 20

The next afternoon, Kevin, Danny, Bitsy, and I met in Danny's basement to practice for the talent show auditions. Danny was unusually quiet and despondent. According to Kevin, it was lovesickness.

I taught everyone the chords and the words to "At Seventeen." Bitsy's voice blended well with mine and we were all impressed. The consensus was that we should have more than one song prepared, so we practiced several old rock and roll songs that were fast and fun to sing, since "At Seventeen" was a slow song and rather depressing.

Bitsy bounced her way through each song. I was beginning to feel uncomfortable, realizing that all eyes in the audience would be on her because she looked so alive and attractive.

"Emily, you need to loosen up," she finally said to me. "I feel silly dancing to the songs while you just stand there like a tree." She straightened the green poppies in her hair. They matched her green sweater. "I don't mean to criticize, but how can you listen to rock and roll music without moving to the beat?"

I knew she was right, and I could tell by the look on Kevin's face that he did too.

"Let's try it again," Bitsy continued, "and this time, Emily, *feel* the song as you're singing it, and just move the way the song tells you to move." She bounced in place a couple times to show me what she meant.

"But aren't we going to have microphone stands?" I argued, thinking I would have to stand still because of that. Singing in front of an audience was one thing, but dancing in front of them was another.

"We can pull the mikes off the stands, so we're free to move around," she explained.

Danny disappeared for a minute, then returned with two empty Coke bottles. "Here," he said, thrusting them at us. "Pretend these are mikes."

I felt stupid at first, dancing around Danny's basement and singing into an empty Coke bottle. But all of a sudden, I began to feel like I did when I was giving my speech. Once I got into it, I forgot all about myself. Actually, it felt more comfortable to move around than to just stand still while I was singing. Imagine, I thought, Bitsy teaching Crocker how to be bouncy. Killion would like that. I felt a sudden pang of regret as I thought about Killion. I missed sharing little things like that with her.

We took a break and Kevin and Bitsy disappeared upstairs together. Danny found some Coke bottles that weren't empty for us to drink. I sat on the couch, petting Ginger, the cat. Danny joined me, sulking.

"You're not your usual crazy self today, Dan," I joked, trying to lighten things up a little.

"So what else is new?" he answered in a monotone voice.

"It's Killion, isn't it?"

He shrugged. "I got this yesterday." He tossed me his invitation to Jacob's party. "He and I used to be good friends, you know. I feel obligated to go to his party, but . . ."

"But not if Killion is his date," I finished for him.

Danny slid off the couch to sprawl out on a braided rug on the floor. He seemed thoughtful. "You know, Em, I could handle her going out with him if I didn't feel . . ." He hesitated. "If I didn't feel that she cares about *me*."

He rolled over onto his stomach. "You see, I get these vibrations every time I'm around her." He paused, glancing up at me. "Do you think I'm crazy? You think I'm inventing signals between us that just aren't there?"

I shook my head no, feeling sorry for him but resisting

the urge to tell him what Killion had secretly confessed to me.

He went on. "Whenever our eyes meet, she doesn't look away. I feel like she's subtly trying to tell me she likes me, or to just hang in there, or *something*. But I can't ever get her away from Jacob long enough to find out." He paused for a moment. "Besides all that, she acts so *different* around him. I don't know what it is. She's so into his money."

"You noticed," I agreed.

He yanked the invitation off the couch and flipped it irritably across the room. Ginger sprang off my lap to track it down.

"I can't go to that party." Frowning up at me, he asked, "Are you going?"

I chuckled. "Oh, you must have heard. I'm not high on Killion's list of best friends right now either." I shook my head. "I don't know if I'm going or not."

"I have an idea, Em," Danny began slowly. "If we *do* go to the party, why don't we plan on meeting there? Then, maybe we could put on a act, or do *something* to make Killion jealous, just to see if she really does like me."

Even the thought of "putting on an act" in front of all those people made me nervous. I didn't want to embarrass Mark, or myself for that matter. "No, Danny," I answered, "just trust me. You're right about the vibrations, and I *know* Killion likes you." Then I added quickly, "But I can't tell you any more than that."

He ignored my plea as a slow smile spread across his face. "Make her jealous," he repeated. "The more I think about it, the more I like the idea." He rose up on his knees to think it over some more, smiling even wider. "Please, Em? Can we try it?"

"Danny, I'm too self-conscious around people. I'm not an actress." He looked disappointed. "I'm sorry, but I could never do anything like that, and please don't try to make me."

He slumped down on the floor as Ginger leaped onto his

lap. He ruffled her fur. "Okay, Em, it was a rotten idea. Just forget it."

Kevin and Bitsy reappeared, with their arms around each other. We continued our practice session until we all felt confident enough to face the upcoming audition. The flirtation between my brother and my new friend was getting pretty heavy by the time we all went our separate ways.

Later that night at home, lying on my bed and listening once more to my song, I couldn't help thinking of both Killion and myself every time this chorus came around:

"Remember those who win the game
lose the love they sought to gain. . . ."

It seemed like both of us had been so busy trying to achieve some elusive dream that we'd missed out on a potentially good relationship that was right in front of us—if we would only open our eyes and look. For Killion it was Danny, and for me, Mark. I'd finally seen the light and I hoped Killion would, too.

I decided I might have cared about Austin if he'd been a little more like Mark. Or maybe, a lot more like him. My thoughts rested on Mark. He was too perfect. I couldn't find anything wrong with him. A strange feeling tugged at my insides and I started wishing all those things Austin had said to me at the mall had been said by Mark instead.

Chapter 21

Losing your best friend and your boyfriend all in one weekend would be bearable only if two new relationships were begun to replace them. I could never replace Killion as a best friend, although it was nice getting to know Bitsy. But I could replace Austin with Mark. That one was easy.

Bitsy and I started eating lunch together, which was all right with me. Then Kevin and Danny began to join us every day. I was right about Michael Farrah and Bitsy. They'd had a "lover's quarrel." She was going to Jacob's party with Kevin.

Killion continued to eat with Jacob, but many times I noticed her watching us. I tried to smile and wave at her, but she always looked away. I really missed her and wondered if she missed me, too.

My friendship with Bitsy was growing, but it was a surface relationship, somewhat superficial. We would never be deep, lifelong friends the way Killion and I were. Or at least the way we had been. Bitsy didn't confide her inner thoughts to me. She never mentioned Michael Farrah either. I wondered if she sensed I had more than a casual interest in him. There was really no way she could know, but sometimes I felt like it was written all over me. I also felt I had to watch what I said around her and that she would think I was weird if I tried to confide in her. Sometimes I even wondered if we would've become friends at all if she hadn't had her eye on my brother.

One night after school, Bitsy and I scrounged through our closets to find matching outfits we could wear in the talent show. We came up with boots, blue jeans, and red turtleneck sweaters. To top it off, Bitsy promised to pick up some red carnations from her Uncle Lebowitz's store for us to wear in our hair the night of the show. I was a little skeptical, but Kevin and Danny thought it was a great idea.

The audition was a breeze. After listening to a few acts that were just so-so, I lost my nervousness because I knew we were much better. Having three of my friends up on the stage with me helped a whole lot, too. Our act got a lot of applause and we knew right away that we'd made it. We were going to be billed on the program as "Crocker and McGee."

Jacob had rounded up a group of guys and formed a band of his own at the last minute. All the equipment belonged to him, and it was impressive, but the group just didn't have it together yet. One of the guys got a couple of girls he knew from the university to sing with the group. It didn't sound as if they'd even rehearsed at all. Why did I get the distinct feeling that the whole thing was put together just to show us up? I noticed Killion wasn't even there to watch the auditions. I also noticed Jacob was getting obnoxious over one of the college girls.

Nowadays at school I was beginning to see more and more of Mark. He'd either be at my locker first thing in the morning or he'd leave me a note. I looked forward to seeing him every day and was always a little disappointed when I found a note instead of him—even though the notes were always great.

The staff at the clinic was having a Christmas party the same night as Jacob's party. Mark invited me to go with him and I said yes. Then, on second thought, I asked him if we could divide the evening in half and stop by Jacob's party, too. I sure hoped Killion and I had made up by then, because I knew I'd feel really awkward going to the party and having her ignore me all night.

That afternoon I hurried home after school. Kevin and I were planning to make our annual trip to the mall to go Christmas shopping. I was eager to talk to him because he'd promised me he'd try to corner Killion some time during the day to see if he could help straighten things out between her and me. Kevin and Killion had practically grown up together as brother and sister, and I knew Kevin could cut through all the small talk and get Kill to level with him.

I found Kevin and his sorrowful-looking car sitting in front of the house when I got home. I ran inside to dump my books, yell hello and good-bye to Mom, give a quick kiss to Wendy, grab a handful of Christmas cookies, and tear back out the front door.

"Whew!" I puffed as I hopped into the car. "I don't know how much longer I can survive this hectic pace. Between school, the clinic, rehearsals, Mark, and Christmas—it's crazy."

"Feel like you're living in a Dr. Pepper commercial?" Kevin joked.

"Exactly. But please don't ask me to get out of the car and go dancing down the street. I just couldn't!"

It felt good to laugh. My life seemed to have gotten so serious all of a sudden.

As Kevin impatiently urged his car down the street, I gave him the third degree about Killion, and he told me what had happened.

"She got a pass to go to the library during study hall time, so I got one, too. Then I ambushed her behind the periodicals and quickly escorted her into an empty conference room and closed the door for privacy. She was pretty insulted at first, but I finally got her to talk."

"And?"

"And, to make a short story long, she's basically mixed up."

"What's the problem?"

"She admitted to me she cares about Danny. A lot."

"That seems to be common knowledge." I couldn't keep the sarcasm out of my voice. "So why is she being so exclusive with Jacob?"

"Money."

"That's ridiculous."

"No. Here's what's ridiculous." He emphasized each word, "She wants to get married to Jacob."

"Get married?" I scooted up to the edge of the car seat, accidentally banging my head against the low roof. "You're kidding!"

"No. Don't get me wrong, though. She doesn't want to get married right away. She just wants to hang on to him. Her plan is to get an engagement ring for high school graduation and a wedding ring for college graduation."

"Her *plan?*"

"Yeah. It's something she got from a book called *The Romance Plan.*"

"Oh, no," I groaned, rubbing the bump that was forming on my head. "She's planning her life after one of her romance novels? I should have known she'd do something that corny. How does Jacob feel about—The Plan?" I asked.

"That's the funny part. He apparently doesn't know anything about it."

"What?"

"According to the book, it's *her* plan—and I quote— 'She slowly reveals it to him as their relationship progresses,' " Kevin said, imitating Killion's voice. "If she does it right, he'll think the whole thing was his idea."

"According to the book," I repeated sarcastically. "Sounds like it was written in the dark ages. Does the book say what to do if the guy goes out with other girls behind your back?"

"You're kidding!" Kevin exclaimed. "Jacob's going out on her?"

I nodded.

"Does she know?"

"I don't think so." I sighed. "She's really crazy. She cares about Danny and she wants to *marry* Jacob?"

I searched Kevin's face, looking for an answer, but he only shrugged.

"She's got to stop taking romance novels literally. She's basing her life on some author's imagination." Between the bump on my head and Killion, I was getting a headache. "I'll bet her dad has a lot to do with this, too," I said softly. "I know he's strict with her and she feels unwanted sometimes, but I didn't know it bothered her this much." I remembered Killion's comment, "You just don't understand how hard it is living at home right now." Had her dad been trying to keep her from dating? She hadn't told me. I turned toward Kevin. "Do you think she's doing this because of her dad? Or because Jacob's family has a lot of money?"

Kevin answered with another shrug.

I curled up on the seat to think and to keep warm at the same time. Kevin's heater, along with just about everything else on his car, didn't work.

"I'm in shock," I said to him. "But what does all this have to do with her not speaking to me?"

"I think, and this is just my opinion," Kevin answered, "that she's avoiding us—her friends—because she knows we'd react just the way we're reacting. We'd all think she was crazy and we'd try to talk her out of it. Plus," he added, looking over at me, "she thinks you and Bitsy are best friends now and that you've dumped her."

"What?" I sat up straight. *"She's* the one who stopped speaking to *me.* I can be friends with other people besides her if I want to. Killion's my *best* friend. Doesn't she know that?"

My answer was another shrug. He wasn't being very helpful.

Kevin's attention was diverted by the crowds of shoppers at the mall. His car jerked up one row and lurched down another as he tried to find a place to park.

"Why does Christmas always come when the stores are so crowded?" he grumbled. "By the time I find a place to park, the holidays will be over."

We agreed on a time and a place to meet, then went our separate ways. Kevin called out after me, "Remember, Em, all I want for Christmas is a small radio—with a brand-new car wrapped around it!"

Chapter 22

I couldn't concentrate on my shopping list after what Kevin had just told me about Killion. I wanted to grab her and shake some sense into her. There was no way I was going to let my best friend continue to make a fool out of herself over some guy who obviously didn't take their relationship seriously. Especially when dear, sweet Danny was crazy about her.

The heroine with "The Plan" in Killion's newest romance novel didn't seem to have as much sense as Loralee. Killion herself even said that Loralee would have picked Danny over Jacob. What was wrong with her? I thought back to something she'd said during our fight that now made sense to me: "With Jacob I've got a chance to change my life. . . ."

In the mall, I found myself being pulled along with the crowd. I grabbed a spot on a half-empty bench so I could sit down for a while to gather my thoughts. All of a sudden I saw the words to my song applying more to Killion than to me:

> "The rich-relationed hometown queen
> marries into what she needs
> with a guarantee of company
> and haven for the elderly. . . ."

"Hi ya!" A sudden loud voice made me jump. "Is there room for me on your bench?" I looked up to see Danny. He squished in beside me.

"I want to show you a present I bought for somebody

special, just in case that somebody special is speaking to me again by the time Christmas rolls around."

"Oh, Danny, that's sweet of you."

He opened a box and showed me a small gold friendship ring. "Isn't it bee-yoo-ti-ful?"

I got a lump in my throat. I didn't have the heart to tell him about Killion's Plan. It would really hurt him. "It's very nice," I answered.

"Nice? No, it's not just nice. It's bee-yoo-ti-ful. Say it with me." He clamped his hand under my chin and squeezed in my cheeks.

"Bee-yoo-ti-ful!" we said together, laughing.

"Hey," he said, "this is the most expensive ring five dollars can buy!"

"Oh, Danny, you can always make me laugh. Killion is going to love it. I know she will."

"Yeah. She'll probably laugh when she sees it. Then she'll show me one that somebody else gave her that's fourteen-karat gold and has a million diamonds in it."

I didn't know what to say, so I changed the subject. "What's in here?" I asked, opening up another one of Danny's purchases. It was a large blue stuffed walrus with sad eyes.

"Ohhhh, is this for your little brother?" I crooned.

"Naw," answered Danny, looking embarrassed. "He's not getting anything from *me* this year. Not after what he gave me for Christmas last year."

"What'd he give you?"

"Strep throat."

I hugged the walrus, then put it back into the sack. "Danny, I think I'm going down to Mr. Lebowitz's store to see if Killion's working right now so I can talk to her. I'll see you later, okay?"

"Can't I come too?" He had a pleading look in his eyes.

"You want to?" I was afraid Killion might ignore him.

He nodded. "Let's go."

Even though the mall was so crowded you could barely walk, there were only a handful of customers in Mr. Lebowitz's store.

"My store's always this crowded before Christmas," he said, rolling his eyes.

I introduced him to Danny and asked for Killion.

"Ay, you kids just missed her. She left early so she could help a friend get ready for a Christmas party he's having tomorrow night."

Danny and I exchanged glances. "Thanks, Mr. Lebowitz," I said as we turned to leave.

"Wait, Miss Emily."

I turned back and he motioned for us to come closer. "Now, this is probably none of my business, but I know you two are good friends, and I want to tell you—I'm worried about Angel."

"Why?" Danny and I both asked together.

He hunched his huge shoulders over the counter and leaned on his elbows. "She's been moping around here for days. Something is very wrong, but she won't tell me what it is. I even found her crying in the back yesterday. Since you're her good friend, I thought you should know." He reached over and patted my hand.

It seemed too long a story to explain to him, so I just thanked him again and decided on the spur of the moment to buy something. I picked out an interesting-looking plant and an I-miss-you-type friendship card to take by Killion's house so it would be there when she got home later. I really wanted her to know I was still her friend if she needed me, and that I wasn't mad at her.

When I got home I hurried to my room to play a new record that I'd bought for myself. I put "At Seventeen" back into its jacket and tossed it onto the top shelf of my closet. All of a sudden that song seemed silly to me. I didn't feel gloomy, and the lyrics didn't seem to relate to me anymore. I decided that when I sang the song in the talent show, it would be for the last time. How symbolic, I thought as I sprawled on the bed.

I felt happy and sad at the same time. Sad about Killion, but happy about the upcoming events. Thursday night was Jacob's party and the clinic's party, too. Mark and I would be going on our first formal date together. I was beginning to feel like Mark's girl. I wanted to *be* Mark's girl.

Plus, I was sure Killion would be friendly to me when I saw her at Jacob's house. She just had to forgive me and make up. We'd been best friends too long to let a guy come between us.

Then Friday night was the talent show where "Crocker and McGee" would be making their debut. I wasn't even scared—just excited.

Suddenly Kevin knocked on my door. "Nice to hear some decent music coming from your room for a change!" he called. "If you can tear yourself away, you have a phone call."

I followed him back down the hallway.

"Hello?"

"Emily? Hi. This is Michael Farrah."

I swear my heart stopped completely. "M-Michael Farrah?"

"Yeah. You know, from English class?"

Was he kidding? Of course I knew.

"Hope I'm not calling too late." He paused as the thought flashed through my mind: Yeah, about ninety-five years too late . . .

He continued. "I was wondering if you'd like to go to Jacob's party with me tomorrow night?"

Silence. I couldn't believe that Michael Farrah was finally asking me out! And I was going to tell him *no!*

"Emily?"

"Yes, Michael. Um, thank you so much for calling. I . . . uh . . . I'm sorry, but I already have a date for tomorrow night."

"Oh, I see." He paused again. "How about the next night? After the talent show?"

I couldn't believe it. I swallowed a giggle. "Sorry again. I'm afraid I already have a date for that night, too."

"Well, maybe some other time."

"Sure. Maybe."

We said good-bye and I flew back to my room, collapsing on the bed, half laughing and half crying.

I looked around my bedroom. Michael Farrah had asked me out and nothing had changed. The record was still playing. The closet door was still standing open. The bedspread was still scrunched up where I'd been lying. Everything was just as I'd left it.

I felt a strange calmness come over me. I must really care about Mark, I thought, because he just passed the ultimate test—getting chosen over Michael Farrah.

Chapter 23

In all the excitement of the last few days, I'd almost
forgotten Thursday was my birthday. Sweet sixteen. Mom
made me open my birthday present early so I'd have a new
outfit to wear to the two Christmas parties. It was a
wine-colored silky blouse and black velvet slacks. She'd
even bought matching accessories so I'd be all set. I felt
another pang of regret, though, when I opened the wine-
colored pierced earrings. Mom knew Killion and I had
planned to go together and get our ears pierced, then give
each other earrings for Christmas. I tucked them away in
the back of a drawer, hoping wistfully that I could wear
them sometime before Christmas.

On the spur of the moment, I'd invited Mark over for
my birthday dinner, which I was going to prepare. Now I
was beginning to question whether that rash impulse had
been a sane thing to do. I'd found a good recipe in my
beginner's cookbook for old-fashioned spaghetti sauce, and
had gotten up early to start it in a crock-pot so it could
simmer all day to blend the flavors. I didn't know it was
going to take ninety-five years to chop up tiny pieces of
onion, green pepper, garlic cloves, and black olives, or
that chopping onions was going to make my mascara run
and leave a permanent odor on my hands. Afterwards, I had
to run all the way to school to make it on time.

Mark was not waiting for me at my locker, and the note
I found looked like it'd been scribbled in a hurry:

Emily, Where are you? You're late. I can't wait
until tonight. I'll be thinking about you all day. Love,
Mark P.S. Happy Birthday.

I got goose bumps when I saw that he'd signed it "Love."

It seemed like the day was over in minutes instead of hours. After school, Crocker and McGee and company met briefly to rehearse one last time before the talent show. We were in top form and our spirits were high.

I tore Kevin away from Bitsy because he'd promised me a ride home after school so I could shower and dress in a hurry, then get back to work on my dinner.

Garlic bread was easy, and another half hour of chopping vegetables resulted in a lopsided tossed salad and two bleeding fingers. Not bad for a first try, I guess.

Mark arrived early, which got me rattled. I let the tea boil over instead of steep, and the garlic bread came out crustier than I'd planned, which wasn't convenient for people who wore braces.

Mom stayed out of the kitchen, saying she was trying the "sink or swim" method in my training as a cook, but she did jump in and save me at the last minute when she saw I was sinking rather than swimming.

I was all out of the mood to eat by the time dinner was ready. But I still had five rolls of breath mints if I got hungry later. Everyone complimented me and no one even mentioned the pasty spaghetti. Kevin even said it tasted so good it made him want to speak Italian. But the only word he knew was "Rome."

I watched Mark as he ate. He looked so handsome tonight, wearing a navy sports jacket over a blue sweater and a checkered shirt. He seemed uneasy around my family, but he kept winking at me while Dad talked to him about the clinic. He ate three helpings of spaghetti, then asked about dessert.

"Dessert!" I wailed. "Come back tomorrow night after I've had another whole day to work on dessert." I glared at Kevin in a silent warning not to mention the "fail-proof fudge" recipe I'd tried the day before. The ingredients listed did not include dynamite, which was what it was going to take to get the rock-hard fudge out of Mom's good pan. She'd planned ahead, though, and pulled out a birthday cake she had hidden away.

Mark brought me pink roses, which he gingerly pinned onto my blouse before we left. In the car he made me sit close to him and open my birthday present as he drove. It was a silver bracelet engraved with my initials. I slipped it onto my wrist.

It felt so good to be out with someone I was comfortable with. When Mark and I were together, it seemed like we had ninety-five million things to talk about, which was quite a contrast from Austin and me.

At a red light, he leaned over and kissed me. "Mmmmm. You smell nice. What is it? White Shoulders?"

"No, white onions."

He laughed, but it was true.

The clinic's staff party was held at Jenny's apartment. She was absolutely delighted that Mark and I had come together. Jenny introduced us to the doctors and nurses we didn't already know and to her fiancé, Roger.

"Emily, I have something important to ask you," she said to me as she linked arms with Roger. "After Rog and I are married next month, we're moving away, so I won't be able to teach my exercise class anymore. I want you to take over as the instructor."

"Me?" I loved going to the class, partly because Jenny made it fun. She led the dances from a platform in front of the gymnasium, and her enthusiasm was catching. "You want *me* to be the instructor?" I repeated.

"Yes. I've thought it over and you'd be perfect. You've picked up the movements to every song really fast and you're good. Plus, you're in great shape," she said, winking at Mark. "Your slenderness will be an inspiration to the ladies in the class to keep exercising."

I was flattered that she'd chosen me and intrigued by the idea of being a "teacher."

"The job doesn't pay *real* well, but it's not bad. Will you do it?"

Everyone looked at me, waiting for my answer. "I'll give it a try, but I can't believe I'm going to get paid for having fun."

It was strange being at an adult party and yet being treated as an equal. Mark and I were obviously the youngest couple there. Everyone was having mixed drinks, which they offered to us. I politely refused, and was relieved when Mark did also.

I was surprised to find that adult parties got just as loud as high school parties and some people acted just as crazy. Mark and I danced slow a few times, which was difficult because he's so tall. But I loved the way he picked me up and swung me around at the end of each dance.

Before it got too late, we said good night and headed toward Jacob's party. I felt the apprehension begin as soon as we got into the car. Mark sensed I was tensing up. He pulled me over and drove with his arm around me. I was hoping Killion and I would at least be back on speaking terms by now since I'd delivered the plant and card to her house, but I hadn't heard from her at all. I felt the next move was hers.

The neighborhood Jacob lived in was quite impressive. Branches from huge trees hung over the parkway and partially blocked the view of gigantic houses which loomed high upon the hill.

We drove through tall iron gates and up a long drive to the front of Jacob's house. A valet took Mark's keys and left to park his car as we walked up the marble steps and through the brocaded entryway. When we arrived, someone who looked like a butler announced our names. I could tell Mark was uncomfortable, and I thought it was going a little too far for a mere group of high school kids.

The party was spread out over five rooms. At one end of the house was a large ballroom intended for formal dances. We could walk in a straight line through four other rooms and end up in the kitchen, which in itself was almost as big as my whole house. That's where we found Kevin and Bitsy.

"Can you believe the size of this house?" Bitsy squealed.

I shrugged a shoulder, determined not to be taken in by Jacob's showiness like everyone else.

"It's awesome," Kevin added. "This house is so big, when it's six o'clock in the kitchen, it's seven o'clock in the ballroom."

One of the caterers stopped to offer us some appetizers.

Kevin tried to joke with him, but was ignored by the young man.

"They're all like that," Bitsy whispered to us after he moved on. "Even Jacob's family is so formal."

"Yeah," Kevin agreed. "They make you feel right at home—and that's exactly where you wish you were."

Out of the corner of my eye, I saw Michael Farrah step into the room, look around, then step out again.

"Excuse me." Bitsy smiled sweetly and bounced off in the direction Michael Farrah had disappeared. I noticed the unhappy look on Kevin's face.

"You're lucky you caught us together for an instant," he grumbled. "She's been disappearing every two seconds all night." He swallowed an appetizer in one bite and headed off in another direction.

Mark and I got something to drink. He found some friends he knew from school, so I slipped away to see if I could find Killion. I found Jacob first and was not surprised to see him with his arm around one of the college girls who'd been recruited to sing with his group in the talent show.

I wandered all the way to the ballroom before I found Killion. I was sure she'd seen me come through the large double doors, yet she made no attempt to acknowledge my presence. She was standing on a low stage next to the band, talking to an older couple who were, I assumed, Jacob's parents. Disgusted with her, I turned to leave and bumped into Danny. He had his jacket on.

"Danny!" I exclaimed, raising my voice so he could hear me over the crowd. "Where are you going?"

"I'm leaving."

"Why?"

He nodded in Killion's direction. "She doesn't even know I'm here. She's spent the evening talking to Jacob's parents, while Jacob's off in another room with . . ."

"I know."

"Hey, Em," Danny began as he pulled me over to the wall and away from the crowd. "Remember when we talked about doing something tonight to make Killion jealous?"

"Danny, we canceled that plan, remember? I told you I'm not an actress."

"I know, but just listen to my plan."

"Danny." I groaned, rolling my eyes.

"Just listen," he repeated, putting a finger over my lips. "Killion reads romance novels, right?"

"How'd you know about that?"

"Kevin told me she believes every one of those books she reads and patterns her life after them."

"So?" Killion would die, I thought, if she knew that Danny knew.

"So I read one of them."

"You did?" The thought of Danny reading one of Killion's romance novels struck me funny and I started to giggle.

"Come on, Em, don't laugh. Consider it research."

He waited patiently until my giggling spell passed, then continued, "The book was called *Jealous Suitor* and guess what? There was a scene at a party—just like this party— where the guy dances with the girl's best friend. It makes the girl insanely jealous and they end up getting together by the end of the book."

"They always get together by the end of the book," I pointed out.

"The thing is, Em, if Killion really does pattern her life after these books, she'll fall for it."

"How do you you know she's even read that particular book?"

"I checked it out from the school library. Her name was on the card."

"Clever," I said, considering the idea. "So all we have to do is dance together? And let Killion see us?"

"Right."

"It's not going to work on Killion, Danny, I—"

"Just try it," he interrupted.

I glanced around for Mark, but he wasn't in the ballroom. I was sure he wouldn't mind me dancing once with Danny. "Well, I think your idea is ridiculous, but I'll try it, if you insist."

"Great. We've got to work fast. I don't want her to

think I'm stupid enough to come to this party alone and get ignored by her. Come on!''

Danny pulled me onto the dance floor and we began to dance slow, even though there was a fast song playing. He wrapped his arms around me, nearly crushing me. Everyone around us began to stare. Suddenly Danny lifted my chin and started kissing me passionately—right in front of everybody!

''Danny,'' I gasped, pushing him away. ''Is this what you call dancing?''

He smothered me with another kiss. I thought I was going to die of embarrassment. Another song started and Danny kept such a tight hold on me, I couldn't have stopped if I wanted to. I was almost afraid to open my eyes and see who was observing this sudden display of affection between Danny and myself. I spotted Kevin, still alone. He leaned against the far wall, with a smirk on his face as he watched everyone else watching us. Danny must have told him what he was planning to do tonight.

When I caught his eye, I thought he was trying to tell me something, but I didn't quite understand the message. I decided to tell Danny I'd had enough so I could get back to the kitchen and find Mark, who was probably beginning to wonder what had happened to me by now.

Then I spotted Killion. She stood there wide-eyed, staring at us. She looked shocked, but I couldn't tell from her expression whether or not she was bothered.

''I think it's working!'' I gasped again into Danny's ear. I was beginning to wonder if he was enjoying this act a little too much.

''I know,'' he whispered back. ''Listen, I'm going to dance you over into the corner where she can't see us very well.''

I followed as he led, but thought he was getting a little carried away. He started kissing my neck and running his hands up and down my back. Then he hugged me so tightly, I could scarcely breathe.

When we got just out of Killion's line of view, we started dancing v-e-r-y slowly. Some of the other couples had actually stopped dancing just to watch us in amazement.

"Danny, don't you think this is enough? I've got to go now. I need to get back to—"

"Not yet!"

Suddenly Danny pulled me down onto a nearby love seat, wrapped his arms around me, and pretended to gaze fervently into my eyes. It was hard for me to keep a straight face, and I had to look away. I noticed Kevin trying to work his way through the crowd toward us. He had a worried look on his face. Directly behind him, Killion had come into view. She'd moved so she could continue to watch us. Jacob was with her now. He was pointing at Danny and me and laughing. Others near them joined in the laughter. Killion looked mad, then she turned on Jacob and it looked as if they were having an argument.

Kevin stopped briefly to watch the commotion they were causing, then continued on his way toward us. He must have been coming to tell us Killion had definitely been convinced by now, or maybe he thought his best friend was getting a little too carried away with his little sister.

He finally made it to where we were sitting. "How are we doing, Kev?" I laughed. "You think she's seen enough?"

"No, Em. I think *Mark's* seen enough."

"WHAT?"

"I've been trying to catch your attention to tell you. He saw the whole thing."

"He couldn't have. I left him in the kitchen—ninety-five miles away from here!"

"Sorry, Em, but he came into the ballroom right after you and Danny started to dance."

For an instant I froze. I couldn't stand the thought of Mark watching what I had been doing with Danny. I jumped up and searched the room for his tall frame.

"Kevin," I said, moaning. "Why didn't you go over to Mark and explain to him what was going on?"

"He was clear across the room. I couldn't get to him fast enough through all these people. Besides, I was a lot closer to you. I tried to signal, but obviously you didn't get the message."

Danny stood up next to me and put his hand on my shoulder. "Em, I'm sorry." He grimaced. "I didn't even know you were with a date tonight."

I brushed his hand off my shoulder, unable to answer him, and started making my way through the crowded room toward the door, noticing briefly that Killion was on her way toward Danny with a strange look on her face.

I spotted Mark by the double doorway. He towered over the people around him. Our eyes met, and I felt sick when I saw the look on his face. It was a mixture of disgust and disbelief.

Frantically, I tried to climb through the crowd to get to him, but he turned and vanished. I thought he'd gone back into the kitchen, but by the time I got there, I realized that he must have left the party completely. Running out the front entryway, I saw his car disappearing over a hill.

I panicked. How could this be happening? Slipping back inside, I slumped against the wall. What should I do? I've got to find Kevin, I thought as I started through the crowd again.

Catching a glimpse of blond hair caught back with a cluster of daisies on the side, I headed in that direction, hoping to find Kevin and Bitsy. I found Bitsy all right, but she was standing with her arms around Michael Farrah. What was she doing? How could she come to a party with my brother, then hook up with another guy when Kevin wasn't looking? Even if it was Michael Farrah, what a rotten thing to do!

I slipped around a corner so they wouldn't see me. Rotten is right, I thought as I realized that's exactly what I'd done to Mark tonight. I mean, that's exactly what he *thought* I'd done.

Kevin found me instead. "Did you find Mark?"

"He left." I started to cry.

"Come on, Em, I'll take you home."

"What about Bitsy?" I sobbed.

He was hurt. I could tell by his face. "Bitsy who?" he mumbled as he steered me back toward the door.

"Wait," I tried to sniff the tears away until I was far

from the party. "I've got to find Danny and tell him that it's not his fault."

"Too late," Kevin answered. "He left, too."

"Oh, no." I started sobbing again.

"No, Em, you don't understand. He left with Killion."

Chapter 24

I must have cried myself to sleep. I don't remember anything until the alarm jarred me from my thankful escape of slumber in the morning. I rolled over and buried my head under the pillow.

What happened after the party was hazy in my mind because I'd been so upset. Kevin had driven me to Mark's house, but his car wasn't there. I'd called him when I got home, but got no answer. Where could he have gone?

Here came the tears again. Austin hated me. Killion hated me. And now Mark hated me. I wasn't too crazy about myself right now either. Merry Christmas, Emily Crocker, I thought.

"Hon? Did you forget to get up this morning?" Dad's voice came through my door. "Today's the big day for your singing debut, isn't it?"

Don't remind me, I thought, pulling the pillow off my head and sitting up slowly.

"Are you in there?" he called. When he got no answer, he stuck his head in the door. "Wow, you look like you had a late night. Must have been a great party!"

"Yeah, great." My voice cracked and my throat hurt from crying so much. My singing voice is going to sound scratchy and terrible tonight, I thought.

Dad left and I dragged myself out of bed. My face looked like it had gained about five pounds overnight, it was so swollen from the tears. My eyes were so full of red lines, they looked like road maps.

I showered and dressed, using the philosophy that wearing a favorite outfit would cheer me up whenever I felt depressed. I put on my rainbow sweater and jean skirt and stood before the mirror. Other than the gloomy look on my face, I thought I looked pretty good. My clothes fit nicely now that I'd gained a little weight, and thanks to the exercise classes, it had all been added in the right places. My skin had responded well to the medication. I hadn't realized how much clearer it was now until I'd run across some old photographs of myself from last summer, which I had stashed in my desk.

Well, that's two goals I've reached from my list of self-improvements. Wait, maybe three goals if I count cooking. I'm not great yet, but at least I'm not afraid of accidentally poisoning anyone now. Oh, I forgot about my hair. Maybe I can cross off the whole list—except for getting a gorgeous tan.

I did a pirouette in front of the mirror, then stuck my tongue out at my image. I always thought that reaching the goals on my list would make me feel deliriously happy. Obviously I was wrong.

I didn't really expect to find Mark waiting at my locker when I got to school, but at least I was hoping for a note. No such luck.

School was a joke. No one took the last day before Christmas vacation seriously anyway, and we ended up playing silly games in most of my classes. I was in such a bad mood, I couldn't even relax and have a good time. The only bright spot in the whole day was during fourth period when my driver's ed teacher took me to get my driver's license.

I skipped lunch. I just didn't think I was in the mood for jokes today. Jokes from whom? That's right, I thought, no one's even speaking to me. Kevin wore a long face today too, and Danny was the last person in the world I wanted to run into. I just couldn't face him because I felt so ridiculous about what we'd done last night.

During English class, Bitsy seemed cool and remote, and Michael Farrah didn't speak or even look at me. I guess I must have injured his male ego. I was worried about Bitsy, though. We all still had to somehow get through the talent show. Oh, how I wished it was all over and done with so I could just disappear over Christmas break.

At home after school, I wasn't in any hurry to get ready for the talent show. I wandered into the kitchen to watch Kevin, who was wrapping some presents. Neither one of us felt like talking.

Mom appeared, holding Wendy, who was noisily sucking her thumb. "'Tis the season to be jolly. What's wrong with you two?" she asked.

We both shrugged our shoulders at the same time.

She continued. "Did you see the two giant candy canes Grandmother Crocker sent over for each of you?" She nodded to one on the table, and I reached for it.

"Hold it!" Kevin snapped. "That one's mine."

"Oh." I pulled my hand back. "Where's mine?"

"I ate yours."

I almost felt like smiling. "Oh, Kev, you're starting to act like your old self again. Come on and see if you can make me laugh. Please?"

"Mmmmm." He accepted the challenge, glancing around the room, looking for ideas. His eyes rested on Wendy. "Do you know why babies suck their thumbs?"

"No." I was already smiling in anticipation of his punch line. "Why do babies suck their thumbs?"

"Have you ever tasted baby food?" He screwed up his face to make his point.

"Oh, big brother," I said, laughing more at his face than his dumb joke. "I'll help you get through tonight if you help me."

"It's a deal." He finished wrapping the last package, then reached into his pocket. "Oh, before I forget, here's the key to my car. Danny's picking me up in a few minutes. We're going over to the school early to help set up the stage and move equipment." He shoved the keys toward me. "I thought I'd let you try out your new driver's license tonight and see if it works."

I stared at him.

"I'm serious. I want you to drive my car since Mom and Dad won't be going to the school until it's time for the show to start, and . . ."

He left off the end of the sentence. I was grateful that he'd stopped before reminding me I no longer had a date with Mark for tonight.

"You're going to let *me* drive your car?"

"Why not? I'm sure you won't do any damage to it. And even if you did, how could I tell?"

"Ooo-kay. Whatever you say. Just remember it'll be the first time I've ever driven alone."

I ate a few bites of leftover spaghetti and changed into my "costume" for the evening—the red turtleneck, blue jeans, and boots that Bitsy and I had chosen. I wondered if Mark was even going to show up tonight. I'd felt nervous only because he was going to be in the audience, but now he probably wouldn't be there at all. I didn't feel relieved, though; I wanted him to be there. I wanted him to be proud of me. Oh, please don't hate me, Mark.

It was late when I finally left the house. I was glad that Kevin had given me his car to drive because it was snowing heavily, and if I'd walked, it would have ruined my hair. But I knew I should have allowed extra time because of the slick streets.

I decided to go the back way because I didn't have much driving experience, and I wanted to stay as far away from other cars as I could.

Suddenly a cat darted right out in front of me. I swerved to miss it and ran the front end of the car up onto the curb. After my heart started beating again, I angrily flipped the gearshift into reverse. The tires started to spin on the icy pavement, and the car stayed right where it was.

Frantic, I jumped out to see what I could do. I knew I needed to create some traction, so I looked through the car for a shovel. There was nothing I could use.

Finding an empty field across the street, I knelt down and began digging through the snow with my bare hands to the dirt below. Scooping up handfuls of dirt was impossible because the ground was frozen, but I managed to loosen enough dirt with the edge of a rock to sprinkle over the ground in back of the tires. I brushed the mud off my hands and clothes the best I could.

After several tries, I finally coaxed the car slowly back-

wards. It worked and I backed out into the middle of the
street. Here we go at last, I thought as I started to shift the
gears. Stuck! The gearshift was stuck in reverse!

I didn't have time to panic. I was already late for the
talent show, and I prayed that I'd get there before "Crocker
and McGee" was announced. There was only one thing to
do. I had to drive to school backwards.

Chapter 25

By the time I waited for all the cars to clear off the streets along the way to school so I could back down them, the talent show had already begun. I parked the car, feeling guilty about it, and hoped that Kevin knew how to fix the problem so he could drive it home the normal way.

I dashed into the school and heard music coming from the auditorium. Thank heavens our act was scheduled late in the show, I thought. Hurrying down the hallway to my locker, I saw a note stuck in the door! "Oh, thank you, Mark." I sighed out loud. I pulled out my guitar, which was stashed in the locker for Kevin to play, then ran down the hall, trying to unfold the note while juggling the guitar in my mud-caked hands. It was impossible. I stuffed the note into my pocket for later and tore down to the rest room to wash the mud off my hands and clothes.

Slipping into the back of the auditorium where the performers were supposed to sit, I spotted Kevin and Danny. They'd saved me a seat.

"Where've you been?" Kevin whispered. "Did you have any trouble with my car?"

I was afraid to tell him. "Um . . . It just doesn't seem to be running right," I whispered back as I looked around. "Wow! This place is packed!"

"You're right. It's so crowded, even the ushers are standing."

"How much of the show have I missed?"

"Most of it. You even missed Stan Jenson."

"What'd he do?"

"He played Beethoven. Beethoven lost."

"Shhhh!" went the people around us.

When it was almost our turn, we slipped out and went backstage. Bitsy was already there and acted somewhat friendly to me as she pinned the flower in my hair. Of course she had to be friendly.

I lied about not being nervous. I was. Very.

The act before ours ended and the curtain came down. We hurried out onto the stage to adjust the mikes and to get ready. Bitsy and I stood in the middle. Kevin and Danny stood on either side of us and a little to the back. We all looked at each other with fixed smiles on our faces as we listened to Loni Ames announcing "Crocker and McGee."

As the curtain went up, Kevin whispered, "Today, the high school auditorium. Tomorrow, MTV."

As we began the song, I heard my voice shaking as I reached for some of the notes. I relaxed a little when I realized I couldn't see any faces in the audience because of the bright footlights. I kind of hoped I'd spot Mark somewhere in the crowd, but I couldn't see anyone.

The words to my ex-song didn't move me the way they used to. The only line that stuck in my mind as I sang was:

"It isn't all it seems at seventeen. . . ."

As the applause died down, we went on into the rock and roll song. The audience loved it! They even started clapping to the beat as Bitsy and I bounced around the stage.

At the end, we ran off, all grinning from ear to ear and listening to the roar of applause, which didn't die down this time.

Loni Ames appeared. "They want an encore. Can you do another song?"

"You're kidding!" we all yelled together, hugging each other.

"Let's go!" Danny cried, and we ran back onto the stage. I was thankful that we'd practiced another rock and roll song. The lights were dimmed a little this time, so I was able to find Mom and Dad in the audience as we sang, but not Mark. The clapping started once more and I could even see a few kids standing up to dance in the aisles.

We took another bow and left again, slipping out into the hallway to catch our breath and get a drink of water. Michael Farrah appeared and whisked Bitsy off. Kevin didn't even bat an eye.

As I was getting a drink, I heard a familiar voice behind me. "Congratulations! You guys were fantastic!" I straightened up and saw Killion hugging and kissing Danny. Jacob wasn't with her. I noticed she was wearing the gold friendship ring Danny had shown me.

Killion came over to me, holding Danny's hand. Danny just stood there, grinning at me like an idiot.

"Hi, Crocker," she said softly. "You were great up there. Did you get my note?"

"What note?"

"I left a note wedged in your locker tonight."

Oh, no. The note I thought was from Mark was really from Killion. And I'd forgotten all about it. I grimaced. "It's in my pocket. I haven't read it yet."

She looked disappointed. "Why don't you read it now?"

I took it out, unfolded it, and read:

Dear Tarrah, I miss you, too. Thanks for the card and the plant. I'm sorry I've been such a jerk, and I'm sorry I missed your birthday. You're the best friend I've ever had. Thanks for not giving up on me. Break a leg tonight. Love, Ginger

I could barely read it because of the tears in my eyes. We hugged each other for a long time. "Killion, look at you," I sniffed. "You've got cheekbones!"

"I know. Isn't it great? Losing all my friends was better than going on a diet. I've hardly eaten a thing for two weeks. I've lost twenty-two pounds in four months."

"That's great." We kept looking at each other. "Oh, Killion, let's never get mad and stop speaking to each other again, okay?"

She took my arm and pulled me away from the others. "Crocker, you were so right about Jacob. He's all those things you said he was—and more,'' she added, pushing up her glasses and staring at her shoes. "We weren't right for each other at all. I was trying to make it something that it wasn't.'' She stopped and looked up at me. "I made a fool out of myself, didn't I?''

"No, you didn't,'' I said, trying to console her.

"Yes, I did. I thought he was my ticket away from home.'' She shook her head. "I was so stupid. Would you believe Jacob was dating two other girls besides me?''

"Probably.''

She laughed. "I had a long talk with my dad last night about Jacob and Danny, and he actually understood. It was incredible. He even let me cry on his shoulder.''

"That's great.''

"I know. He was all right last night, Crocker. He even told me it's time I started making my own decisions.''

I glanced over and saw Danny watching us. "Look, Killion, I'm sorry about the stupid trick Danny and I played on you last night.''

"Stupid is right.'' She laughed. "Did you really think I'd fall for it?''

"You didn't?''

"Of course not. I know you both too well. Besides, I saw Mark at the party and figured you were with him.''

I hadn't thought of that.

"And on top of everything else,'' she continued, "Jacob started making fun of you two and I just couldn't stand hearing him put down my best friends.'' She sighed. "But you can't blame me too much for going out with Jacob after all that time you spent talking about Austin.'' She narrowed her eyes at me.

"Yeah, we sure know how to attract the *wrong* guys.''

She waved to Danny. "Maybe now we know how to attract the *right* guys, too.''

"Well, one of us does,'' I answered, thinking about Mark.

Killion grabbed my arm and pulled me back toward Kevin and Danny, who'd been waiting patiently. "Say, are you sure you still want to be friends with me?'' she asked. "I thought you'd become the clone of Bitsy McGee when I saw you bouncing around on that stage tonight wearing a flower in your hair.''

I pulled the carnation out of my hair and threw it at her. Then we hugged again. Stepping back, I bumped into someone. It was Mark! For an awkward moment we all stood and stared at each other.

"Well," said Kevin, trying to make conversation. "What do you guys think of the unemployment situation?" He put one arm around Killion and the other around Danny to steer them off down the hall and away from us. "I think the reason so many people are unemployed today is because they don't have jobs." His voice trailed off as they walked away.

He's a good friend for a brother, I thought, feeling a sudden twinge of tenderness for him as I turned my attention back to Mark. "Hi," I said timidly, unable to read his face this time, but knowing he could probably read mine. We both started to speak at the same time, then stopped and laughed.

"I guess I need to do some explaining," I mumbled.

He put his fingers on my lips. "Too late."

"Too late?" I could feel the tears coming back again.

He nodded. "Danny found me late this afternoon over at MacKenzie's. I was on my fourth banana split. When I saw him, I almost punched him out. But he calmed me down and explained all about his little plan to make Killion jealous.''

"I'm so sorry, Mark. I thought all we were going to do was dance—like normal people. I didn't know Danny was going to overdo it so much.''

"Yeah, I still should have punched him out. Then I noticed Killion was waiting for him, and that somehow made it seem okay. Even if his plan didn't work on her, it worked on me, in case you're interested." He winked and put his arms around my waist. "Will you forgive me for walking out on you?''

"Me? Forgive you? It's more like, will you forgive me?''

He picked me up and stood me on a stairway so we were the same height. Then he kissed me. I mean, he *really* kissed me. I wondered how come I could hear fireworks going off in the hallway of the school.

"Oh, Mark Logan." I sighed. "*Je t'adore.*"

He gave me a funny look. "Shut the door?" he asked.

I wanted to be alone with Mark, but we got pulled along with the others who were going Christmas caroling. The air was so cold, it almost took my singing voice away. I looked over at Killion and Danny, smiling at each other. Next to them, Bitsy was snuggling up to Michael Farrah. Well, if I'm going to be Loralee in my next life, I'll have to live another one in which I'm Bitsy McGee.

Face it, Emily "Tarrah" Crocker, I said to myself, you're just you. You're not going to end up beautiful and in love like the girls in Killion's romance novels.

But Mark thinks I'm beautiful, doesn't he? He likes my internals and externals, as Killion would say. I looked up at him. And maybe that warm, wanting-to-be-with-him feeling was what falling in love was all about.

He returned my gaze tenderly. I leaned closer and slipped my hand into his. Suddenly I didn't want to be Loralee or Bitsy. At that moment all I wanted was to be Emily Crocker—not even Tarrah—just me, the terrific singer who taught an exercise-dance class, was an okay cook, and was standing here in the snow, looking beautiful, and falling in love with Mark Logan.

DIAN CURTIS REGAN has lived most of her life in Colorado Springs, Colorado. She received a Bachelor of Science degree in education from the University of Colorado in Boulder and taught elementary school in Denver for two years. She is currently serving as the regional advisor of the West Texas chapter of the Society of Children's Book Writers. Dian writes a column on "Writing for the Juvenile Market" for *Byline* magazine and teaches the same topic at Amarillo College. She spends a great deal of time with her word processor, eating gummi bears and writing for young people.